SO-AFS-969

GUT SHOT

Center Point
Large Print

Also by Wayne D. Overholser and available from
Center Point Large Print:

The Durango Stage
Proud Journey
Pass Creek Valley
Summer Warpath
Fighting Man
Ten Mile Valley
High Desert
The Waiting Gun
Guns in Sage Valley
Ten Feet Tall
Skull Mesa
The Cattle Queen Feud

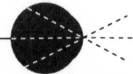

**This Large Print Book carries the
Seal of Approval of N.A.V.H.**

GUT SHOT

Wayne D. Overholser

CENTER POINT LARGE PRINT
THORNDIKE, MAINE

Chapter 1

DAN QUAID finished eating and scooted back his chair, noting that the pendulum clock on the wall behind the cashier's desk showed 1:25, within five minutes of the time he was to meet Sam Wardell. He smiled at his wife Angie, trying to reassure her and knowing he could not. She had been anxious from the time they had sold their Willamette Valley farm near Oregon City, and he had been unable to say or do anything to change her feeling.

His gaze touched the face of their seventeen-year-old son, Johnny. He saw eagerness there, the love of adventure, the impatience stemming from unavoidable delay. Quaid was making this move to Central Oregon for the boy's sake, he told himself, but he wasn't sure. Perhaps it was for himself.

He glanced at Lynn, their daughter who would be nineteen next week. She had been flirting slyly with the cowboy at the corner table, a game she loved and which she had played since she was twelve. Sometimes Quaid wondered whether she would ever grow up and fall in love with a man and settle down. Angie said it was a problem time would solve, that when Lynn did fall in

5

love, it would be for keeps. Quaid hoped that she was right.

He rose and pushed his chair back against the table. He said, "Time for me to go. I don't know when I'll be back."

"I'll wait for you in the lobby," Angie said.

"If I take too long, go up to the room and rest." Quaid nodded at his son. "Stay out of trouble, Johnny."

"Sure," the boy said amiably. "You know I never get into trouble."

"You, too, Lynn."

She winked at him. "I won't guarantee it, Dad. How can you have any fun if you don't get into trouble?"

He grinned at her. He couldn't help it. She had known how to handle him from the time she was a baby. Any discipline she'd received had come from Angie, but perhaps it had been enough. In spite of Lynn's facetiousness and seeming lack of respect, she had an inherent sense of decency that had always kept her out of serious difficulty.

"Try to keep it small trouble," he said and, walking to the cluster of nails near the door, took down the Stetson he had bought that morning and left the hotel.

He paused on the boardwalk, conscious of the stiffness of his new hat and of the fact that it marked him as a greenhorn. This was Prineville on the Crooked River in Central Oregon, as

6

different from the Willamette Valley on the other side of the Cascades as a new world would have been. There the land had been farmed for generations, the way of life old and established, with law and order as certain as it was humanly possible. Here the air was clear and dry and hot on this July day; it filled a man with energy and made him dream big because the land itself was big, with smoldering violence only waiting for an excuse to break into flames.

He smiled as he crossed the street, thinking that it wouldn't take long for his Stetson to shape to his head and become dirty and sweat-stained. He knew how it was in this country, new and still far from developed. He had lived until he was twenty on the John Day not far to the east. Now he felt as if he had come home.

He glanced at the letters on the window of the small frame building across the street from the hotel: Cascade and Eastern Oregon Land Company, Sam Wardell, Agent. Quaid went in, curious about Wardell because they had exchanged a number of letters before Quaid had sold his farm.

Sometimes Wardell's letters sounded as if he didn't care whether Quaid bought land from the company or not. Well, there was plenty of other land around here. Several irrigation projects were going in southwest of Prineville. The railroad being built up the Deschutes would go into Bend, the center of the new irrigated district. Maybe, Quaid thought, he should look at that country before he made a deal with Wardell.

The office was one large room sparsely furnished with a single desk and three chairs. Quaid was surprised. He had expected something more ornate, with a number of bookkeepers and secretaries. The company was big and rich, with many and varied interests besides this one in Central Oregon, so the room didn't seem to represent its wealth and power properly.

The man at the desk rose and walked toward Quaid, his hand outstretched. He asked, "Dan Quaid?"

"That's right," Quaid answered. "You're Sam Wardell?"

"Correct." Wardell gave his hand a hard grip, his gaze taking in Quaid's tall, hard-muscled body. "Funny thing, Mr. Quaid. You form a mental picture of a man you've never seen after you get a few letters from him, but it isn't often that the mental picture fits the real man. Mine came pretty close."

Quaid laughed, wondering where he missed filling the picture. He had formed his mental picture of Wardell, too. He had missed the target only a little. Wardell was older than he had expected, probably sixty although he was well preserved; a tall, straight-backed man in a black broadcloth suit. He wore a diamond ring on his right hand. He had very dark eyes, a glossy black mustache and beard, and hair that was as black except for its streaks of gray. Aside from his age, he was the kind of man Quaid expected to see, personable, good-looking, and prosperous-appearing, but there was a toughness in his eyes and the set of his mouth that Quaid had not sensed in his letters.

"Now I'm curious," Quaid said. "Do I measure up?"

"You do, and more," Wardell said. "You're a bigger man than I expected to see. You must be at least six two and I'd say you weighed around 190 pounds, and you have the look of a man who can take care of himself. That's important, Mr. Quaid, believe me. It's the reason that the offer I made hinged upon a personal interview."

Wardell motioned toward a chair and returned to his desk and sat down. Quaid took the chair and drew his pipe from his pocket and filled it, his eyes on Wardell who had lighted a cigar and was leaning back, his fingers laced behind his head.

"You offered me a particular section of land on Egan Creek above the town of Egan," Quaid said. "The price was two dollars an acre. Now if I like the land and if I have the money, why does the sale depend upon a personal interview?"

"Because I wanted the opportunity to tell you exactly what you're up against," Wardell said.

"I may not always be honest in discharging my duties, but I'm going to be honest with you because it's important for the company. If you had been a soft, fat man or a loud-mouth pipsqueak, I would have told you at once the deal was off."

"Then I'll pass?" Quaid asked, more irritated than he let his face show.

"You will indeed," Wardell said.

"This morning I deposited $5,000 in the bank here," Quaid said, "and in addition I have considerable cash on me. I'll look at the land and if I like it . . ."

"Not so fast, Mr. Quaid," Wardell interrupted. "Not so fast. There are some other considerations. First, I want you to know that we're offering you one of the prize sections in the entire wagon road grant. A few years ago my company bought that part of the grant which extends from the Deschutes River to the Idaho boundary. The price I quote you is ridiculously low. The section I mentioned has 150 acres of bottom land which can be irrigated from the creek and will be the best hay land in the country. In addition, there are about 200 acres of the finest pine timber I have ever seen in my life. The remainder is good grazing land."

Quaid cradled his pipe in his hand, thinking that for some obscure reason Wardell was trying to back out of the deal. He said, "I don't get it.

Why don't you ask what the section is worth?"

"Because you're our guinea pig," Wardell said bluntly. "The company cannot afford to put a man on that land and have him fail. Within the next few years we expect to sell hundreds of thousands of acres and you're our first customer in Egan Valley." He leaned forward, the cigar cocked at a sharp angle between his teeth. "Why do you want to live out there? In other words, why did you give up a comparatively easy life in the Willamette Valley to start here from scratch?"

Quaid took time to light his pipe. Wardell's question was one he had asked himself many times and he wasn't sure of the answer. He said slowly, "I have a seventeen-year-old boy. I know what this country is like and what it does for a man. I wanted that done for Johnny."

"Is that all?" Wardell pressed. "I'm being honest with you. I expect you to be honest with me."

Quaid took his pipe from his mouth and stared at it. There was more, more even than his wife Angie knew, but he did not have it entirely clear in his own mind and he wasn't sure he could make it clear to Wardell.

"Not quite all," Quaid said finally. "I got tired of the rain and mud and fog of the Willamette Valley. I remembered how clear the sky used to be on the John Day and how dry and bracing the air was and how close the stars were at night. I

11

got so I hated the dampness of the Willamette Valley that took the sap out of a man and made him feel as if he didn't care whether he amounted to a damn or not."

He put the pipe back into his mouth and pulled on it, but it had gone cold and he took it out. Then he added, "I'm forty-two, Wardell. I don't know how many good years are ahead of me. I've got to find out."

There was still much that was left unsaid, but Wardell seemed to understand. He smiled and said, "Good. It may surprise you to know that I could sell this section of land to fifty men. Making a quick sale is easy, but planning ahead to long range development of our property is not so easy. That's why I wrote to several men I knew in Oregon City and found out a good deal about you."

Quaid was surprised. He watched Wardell get up and walk to a window and stare into the dusty street, still not understanding. A buyer was a buyer, so what difference did it make what the people in Oregon City thought of him? He heard Wardell ask, "You have more of a family than the son you mentioned?"

"A wife and daughter."

Wardell swung around to face him, chewing hard on his cigar stub as if he was reluctant to ask the question which must be asked. "Now this is the nub of the whole deal. Are you prepared to go into a situation which might cost you your life or the life of your son, and will certainly bring suffering and hardship to your wife and daughter?"

"I don't see any sense in your question," Quaid said. "I just want to buy a section of land."

"Before we go any farther," Wardell said, "I want you to ask a few questions of other people in town. Go to Rufe Langer in the bank. And the sheriff, Billy Mason. Or anyone else you want to. Tell them you have been offered an excellent proposition by me and ask their advice. If you still want the section, come back and see me."

Quaid hesitated. "It isn't necessary. Describe this section to me and I'll ride up there in the morning."

"And maybe never come back?" Wardell shook his head. "Don't be a fool, Quaid. Find out what you're getting into. Tobe Henderson and his oldest boy are in town. I saw them at noon. They're squatters up there. They hate me and the company and anybody who buys from us. If you want a hell of a fight, go ask them about the deal. You'll probably find them in the Stockmen's Bar."

Quaid rose and knocked his pipe out on the ash tray on Wardell's desk. "I will," he said, and left the company's office.

Chapter 2

QUAID went to the hotel first. There he found Angie waiting in the lobby as she had said she would. She rose when she saw him coming and stood waiting, her blue eyes fixed on his face as if trying to read in his expression what had happened. Funny, he thought, that after all these years of marriage, he could look at Angie now and find his heart bouncing and turning just as it had when he'd first fallen in love with her.

"Let's go up to our room," Quaid said.

Angie nodded and, putting her hand on his arm, walked up the stairs beside him. This was her way. She would go with him to the ends of the earth just as she had come here with him. He had sensed that she did not fully approve of this move, but she had not argued with him when he had told her what he wanted to do. Now it was time to tell her all that he knew. If she wanted to back out and return to the Willamette Valley, it had better be done without delay.

He opened the door to their room. They stepped inside and he closed the door behind them, then he led her to a window and stood looking down at her. She asked, "What is it, Dan?"

He didn't answer for a moment. Romantic words that every woman wanted to hear did not come easily to his lips, and he wondered why an attractive woman like Angie who could have had her choice of half a dozen men had fallen in love with him.

Now, at forty, she still had the same slim figure she'd had the day they were married. She had refused to let herself get dowdy as so many farm wives did. Her skin was very fair, and although she had taken care of the chickens and had done most of the garden work, her face had never tanned. Aside from the crow's feet around her eyes and the streaks of gray in her hair, she apparently had been untouched by the years.

"I love you, Angie," he said at last. "Now I'm wondering what I've got you into."

"Tell me about it," she said.

He sat on the edge of the bed and pulled her down on his lap. The trip had been a hard one. They had sold their furniture and stock and equipment along with the farm and taken the train to Portland, then had changed trains to go up the Columbia. They had changed again at Biggs to take the spur from the river to Shaniko. There they had stayed the night in the Columbia Southern Hotel and the next morning had boarded the stage for Prineville, arriving last night. Angie was still tired and he wondered if she should rest before he told her.

"Where are the kids?" he asked.

"The hotel clerk told Johnny they were breaking

horses behind Barlow's livery stable and he went down to watch." She shook her head, smiling. "You can guess where Lynn is. She managed to get acquainted with the cowboy who sat at the corner table at noon. I don't quite know how she did it, but she's as bold as brass sometimes. She changed to her riding skirt and they took a ride somewhere."

"You let her go off with a man she never saw until noon?" Quaid demanded.

"Would you have stopped her?" Angie asked.

"No," Quaid admitted. "I guess I wouldn't. Looks to me like we raised a wild filly. The sooner some man tames her the better."

"You ready to tell me about Wardell?" Angie asked.

"I've got a question first," he said. "Maybe it's what people call a woman's intuition, but there have been times when I thought you had second sight. This move was all my doing. Now I'm wondering. Do you know what's going to happen?"

His big arms were circling her waist and holding her harder than he realized. She pushed his arms away and rose. She walked to the window and stood staring down at the dusty street which was almost deserted at this time of the afternoon.

"I wish you hadn't asked me." She paused, and then said defiantly, "It's a crazy superstition

16

to believe in dreams. If I've guessed what was going to happen once or twice, it was just luck. We both know that, don't we, Dan?"

"Just luck," he agreed. "But what was it you dreamed about coming up here?"

She raised her hands to the casing and gripped it. She asked, "Are you sure you want to know, Dan?"

"Yes."

She closed her eyes. "I dreamed we made the move and bought the section of land on Egan Creek that Wardell wrote you about. After that there was nothing but trouble and suffering and heart aches." She paused, her head bowed, and added in a tone so low he barely heard, "And death."

He rose and went to her. "You want to go back to the Willamette Valley?"

She turned to him and tried to smile. "No. I've known for quite a while you weren't happy there. I guess you have too much turbulent blood in you. This is your kind of country, Dan. If we turned back because of a crazy dream I had . . ." She shook her head at him. "Dan, Dan, we couldn't. We'd be worse than cowards. We'd be idiots."

"Maybe not," he said, and told her about his talk with Sam Wardell. "I don't know what it's all about, but I've got a notion Wardell didn't want to sell to me unless I'd stick. The thing is you're involved as much as I am. So are the kids. If we're going to back out, this is the time. And there are other places to live. I mean, it's crazy to think we have to buy this section on Egan Creek."

"No, it isn't crazy," she said. "At least it wouldn't be crazy for you to look at it. If it is exactly what you want, then it would be crazy not to buy it at the price Wardell is offering it. If you don't look at it, it will haunt you all of your life."

She was right. Sometimes he thought she understood him better than he understood himself. He said, "All right, I'll go see the people Wardell told me to."

She raised her hands to the back of his head and kissed him. She said, "I've been afraid of a lot of things, Dan, but most of them never happened. I think the reason is because you keep them from happening."

He picked her up and carried her to the bed and laid her upon it. He said, "You rest till I get back."

He left the room, closing the door gently behind him. As he walked down the stairs he thought about some of her fears. She had been afraid to go to Portland with him on their honeymoon because she had never been there although she had lived within a few miles of the city most of her life. She had been afraid to have children,

18

but after they were born she was proud of them and of herself for having them. She had hoped for another boy, but something had gone wrong after Johnny was born and she couldn't have any more.

It was a real test of her courage, he thought, for her to go ahead and do the things she feared. That was the way it had been about coming here. She feared the unknown more than anything else. He would never know how much it had cost her to leave her home and church and friends, the safe life she understood and liked, and come here to face this primitive country with its unknown dangers. The dream she'd told him about must have been a nightmare. Probably it had been caused by her fears. It meant nothing. As she had said, belief in dreams was nothing more than superstition.

When he left the hotel, he decided the first move was to see Tobe Henderson and his son. If he had to fight, he had better see how bad it was.

He found the Stockmen's Bar almost empty. Four cowhands had a poker game going at one of the green-topped tables, and two more were drinking at the far end of the bar. Quaid asked for whisky, then he said loud enough for everyone in the room to hear, "I've been talking to Sam Wardell. You know anything about the country around Egan?"

The bartender glanced at the two men drinking

at the other end of the bar, then brought his gaze back to Quaid. He said, "No sir, I don't, but yonder's Tobe Henderson and his son Shep. They live up there. They can tell you anything you want to know." His lips tightened against his teeth in a wicked grin. "Fact is, they're fixing to tell you whether you ask 'em or not."

The two men put their drinks down on the bar and walked toward Quaid. The one in front was about forty, the other perhaps half his age and an almost exact replica of the older man except that he hadn't filled out. Time would take care of that, Quaid thought. He would be the image of his father in another twenty years.

The Hendersons stopped two paces from Quaid, the father's muddy eyes making a study of him. Henderson was a full head shorter than Quaid, but he was blocky, with the thickest shoulders and neck Quaid had ever seen. He had a square chin and a wide face, an unforgiving face, Quaid thought, and he judged Henderson to be the kind of man who, once deciding on a course of action, would follow it unrelentingly to its end because he had no capacity to change.

"So Wardell found another sucker," the older Henderson said.

"Maybe I am a sucker." Quaid held out his hand. "I'm Dan Quaid. I just got into town last night. We lived in the Willamette Valley but we like this country."

Henderson did not offer his hand and Quaid dropped his to his side. Henderson said, "If you like this country, buy some land close to town. Or go up the Ochoco. Just don't do any business with the company. If you do, we'll run you out."

"It's my business if I settle on land I've bought from the company," Quaid said. "I won't deal with Wardell unless he can give me a deed to the land I'm buying."

"No, it ain't your business," Henderson said. "It's ours. It's everybody's who lives up there. Wardell's God-damned company ain't got no claim to any of that land and we don't recognize what they say is their legal right to sell it."

"If the company can furnish me with a deed to the land . . ."

"You listen to me." Henderson's thick forefinger jabbed Quaid's chest. "What the law says is one thing and what's right is something else. The law's on the company's side and the right's on our side. We figger that any man who buys land from that son of a bitchin' company is our enemy and that's the way we aim to treat 'em. If you buy from 'em, we'll burn you out and shoot your cattle and maybe even shoot you."

Henderson tossed a coin on the bar and jerked his head at his son. "Let's get out of here, Shep. Sucker smell always makes me sick." He walked past Quaid to the door, then turned, "Mister, the next time you see Wardell, ask him why he wears that scarf around his neck."

They went out then. Quaid looked at the bartender. "Are they crazy? There is some law in this county, ain't there?"

"Law?" The bartender gave him his wicked grin again. "They're crazy and they're tough, friend. If you move up there on Egan Creek, you'll find out about the law."

"I guess I will," Quaid said, "because that's just what I figure I'll do."

He left the saloon, wondering what the sheriff would say.

Chapter 3

QUAID had expected to find the sheriff a tall, leathery-faced man who looked as tough as a boot heel, but Billy Mason didn't fit that description. He was medium tall and on the pudgy side, with pink cheeks and a round face that might have belonged to a very young man, but he had deep lines around his eyes and the front of his head was completely bald. His age was hard to guess. Quaid finally decided he was over forty.

Mason listened attentively while Quaid told him about his deal with Wardell and what Tobe Henderson had said, but he showed his irritation when Quaid asked him why the law didn't reach to Egan Valley.

"You're new in the country," Mason said, "so I'll overlook what's back of that question. First, you've got to understand that this country ain't the Willamette Valley . . ."

"I know that," Quaid interrupted impatiently. "I lived on the John Day until I was twenty. That was rough country, too, but damn it, a man could live on land he owned without being burned out and having his stock shot and getting himself killed. I don't see why it's any different here."

Mason's pink cheeks turned red. He said, "Now if you'll let me talk, I'll finish what I started

23

to say. The people who live around Egan, the Hendersons and Matt Runyan and Orrie Bean and the rest, form a tight little clique. There's about fifteen families of 'em. Some live on their own land, homesteads they've proved up on, and the rest of 'em squat on company land. That includes the Hendersons. They don't own an acre of land, but they've got a big spread and they've made a lot of money out of land they claim is theirs but actually belongs to the company."

"Well, damn it," Quaid said angrily, "why don't the company run the Hendersons off its land?"

Mason shrugged. "You better ask that question of Sam Wardell. They'll evict 'em in time. Right now I guess the company don't want the publicity. Anyhow, these people all hang together whether they're squatters or own their land. I've made some arrests, but I've never got a conviction. They'll lie for each other when you get 'em on the witness stand and you can't convict a man in any court if you haven't got evidence that holds up."

"But if you know they're guilty . . ." Quaid stopped, realizing that what he was saying was ridiculous.

For the first time Mason grinned at him. "Even in the Willamette Valley I guess you don't convict people on what you know. It's on what you can prove in court, and I tell you we have never been able to prove anything on these people."

"Why do all of 'em stick together the way they do?"

"Partly because they're afraid of Tobe Henderson and his boys," Mason said, "and partly because of a man named Matt Runyan. He's an old bachelor who lives alone. He's an educated man who taught their school for a while and sometimes he preaches to 'em. If the regular preacher don't get there when there's a burying, Matt handles the funeral. He's no doctor, but he knows a good deal about medicine, and he doctors their sick. He's not a lawless man like Tobe Henderson, but he's got a talent for leadership. Those people will do anything he asks. Don't ask me how he does it, but I know from experience that he does."

"Is he a squatter, too?"

"No, that's the funny thing about it. He homesteaded a quarter section up Egan Creek years ago and now he has title to his land, but for some reason Runyan considers it his duty to fight the company and anybody it sells to. He tells his people that as long as they can keep the company from ever actually settling a man up there, they can hold the line, but they're whipped if anybody hangs and rattles because others will come and then the company will move in and evict families like the Hendersons."

"Wardell's sold to other men?" Quaid asked.

"The company has," Mason answered. "Wardell

is pretty new. You're his first. The story I hear is that he's their ace agent and he's been sent here to straighten this mess up. He don't want another failure. That's why he's been cagey with you."

"What happened to the others?"

"One lasted about six months and he actually got a cabin up and built a corral," Mason said. "After two or three beatings, he quit. The rest of 'em didn't last three days."

"And you didn't do anything?"

"I haven't been sheriff all this time," Mason snapped. "I made some arrests, but it's like I told you. I never got a conviction."

"If I go up there," Quaid said, "and get shot or beaten up, I won't get any protection from you?"

"Hell man, I can't stop what's already been done," Mason said in exasperation. "Afterwards if you're still alive and you swear who done it, I'll arrest 'em and throw 'em into jail. They'll be tried, but they'll deny it, and some of the rest will swear they were playing poker that night with the men you claim are guilty and there goes your case. They'll walk out of the courtroom free men just like they've done every time."

Quaid rose, trying to control his temper. He said, "All right. Now suppose I buy this section of land and I fight back. I'll shoot some of 'em and maybe kill a man or two. What happens to me?"

"I'll arrest you," Mason answered. "You'll

be tried and probably hung because every God-damned one of 'em will swear you're guilty whether you are or not."

Tight-lipped, Quaid said, "I'd say it's a hell of a situation."

He stomped out of the courthouse and went to the bank.

Rufe Langer could add very little to what the sheriff had said. "I'm sorry you've got your head set on this deal," Langer told him. "You're the kind of man we want to settle here. The bank prospers as Crook County prospers. The railroad will be finished into Bend within the year. Prineville will have a spur. This country will be opened up and settlers will pour in by the thousands. You're bound to make money on any land you buy around here. I was hoping you'd be interested in locating on the lower river or up the Ochoco."

"You're familiar with this section of land Wardell is offering me?" Quaid asked.

The banker nodded. "It would make you a fine ranch. I'd be the last to deny it."

"You know how much money I deposited this morning," Quaid said. "That's all I have except for the cash I'm carrying, and it'll take that and more to stock a ranch and buy equipment. What would it take to buy an established ranch and stock it?"

Langer nodded, his face thoughtful. "I see your

point. You'd have to borrow money, of course. I can tell you now that we'd be glad to make you a loan."

"No," Quaid said. "I'm not going into debt. I have a right to make the best deal for myself I can. I also have the law on my side. Isn't that enough?"

Langer shook his head. "Not on Egan Creek. Maybe those people are fanatics, but by their lights they're honest. Have you heard how the grant was made in the first place?"

"No. All I've heard is that it was given for the building of a wagon road, and the Cascade and Eastern Oregon Land Company bought it from the original road company a few years ago."

"That's right, but men like Matt Runyan claim it was a fraud because the wagon road was never actually built. Not from the Deschutes River to the Idaho line anyhow. As far as I've been able to find out, they're right. It seems that all the road company ever did was to pound a few stakes, blaze a few trees, and shovel a little dirt on the sides of a gully now and then so a wagon could cross. For that they received alternate sections of land for three miles on both sides of the road. They made it stick, too. Well, some of the early settlers took it to Congress and to the courts. They spent more money on lawyers than they could afford, but they didn't get anywhere. After the litigation was all over and the road company's claim to the grant confirmed, it sold out to the C. and E. O. for a fine profit."

"It doesn't change anything," Quaid said. "Wardell's company bought the land, so it has a right to sell to me and I have a right to be protected by the law."

"True, but you have to face the reality of life in Egan Valley," Langer said. "Now among those early settlers was Tobe Henderson's father. Matt Runyan was among them, too. He was a young man at the time. When he discovered what had happened, he moved up the creek and filed on government land that was beyond the six-mile strip. Old Gabe Henderson wouldn't budge. He had lived on his land for years before it was surveyed and before he knew it was company land. I guess Matt regretted that he gave up what was a fine quarter section on the river. Anyhow, he's been their leader ever since old Gabe died. He considers himself a Messiah. Since he has what he claims is moral right on his side, he swears he'll win in the end."

"He won't," Quaid said.

"No," Langer agreed. "It's all been settled in the courts and they might as well make the best of it, but Tobe Henderson is a kind of half outlaw. He'll kill you without batting an eye if he takes a notion to."

Quaid rose. "Maybe I'm just as stubborn as Henderson, but I'm going up there and have a look. If I like it, I'll buy and I'll fight. Maybe the company never sold to a man who will fight."

"Perhaps. But remember you're one man and there are many of them." Langer rose and shook hands. "Let me say one more thing, Mr. Quaid. If you can see your way clear to examine some property that is not in the trouble area, the bank will back you all the way, but if you go there, we can't do a thing for you."

"I understand," Quaid said, and left the bank.

One thing was plain, Quaid thought as he walked toward the company office. If he bought company land, he would be in the fight of his life. Then his troubled thoughts turned to Angie and Lynn. They would have to stay in Prineville. Johnny would face the trouble with him, but Egan Valley would be no place for the women.

"Dad."

He turned, not noticing until that moment that Lynn and a cowboy were leaving a livery stable across the street. He waited for them, Lynn dancing along, the way she did when she was excited. She was so different from Angie that sometimes he wondered how they could possibly have had a daughter like her. She had dark brown eyes and black hair that held an unruly curl; she was small and straight-backed and very pretty, the perfection of her beauty marred only by a cluster of freckles on both sides of her nose.

But the part of her that made Quaid constantly

marvel was her vitality and love of life. She was always seeking adventure and always finding it. Too, she could see beauty everywhere. She had even seen it yesterday morning when they had crossed the barren, wind-swept Shaniko plains in the stage coach.

Quaid always smiled when he saw her so happy, the juices of life bubbling with the sheer pleasure of just being alive. He loved his son Johnny and worked well with him, but Lynn was different. She was something special, perhaps because she was his first born, or because she was just Lynn, flirty and adventurous and always gambling on something.

Before Lynn and the cowboy were halfway across the street, she called, "Dad, I want you to meet Pete Sloane. He's a real, genuine, dyed-in-the-wool, sixteen-carat cowboy."

Sloane grinned as he stepped up on the boardwalk and shook hands with Quaid. "I'm glad to meet you, Mr. Quaid. I met your wife in the hotel and just now I met your son. I understand you're planning to settle here."

"That's right," Quaid said.

Sloane was a slender, wiry man with a pug nose and blue eyes and curly brown hair that showed under his broad-brimmed hat. He was a typical Eastern Oregon cowboy. When Quaid had lived on the John Day, he had been much the same kind of man, wearing the same kind of clothes. He had even carried a gun on his hip the way Sloane was carrying his.

"We were up there." Lynn pointed to a point of rimrock west of town. "Pete took me. You can see all over. It's the most beautiful country I ever saw."

"You're aiming to look at some company land?" Sloane asked.

"In the morning," Quaid said.

"If you don't mind, I'll ride along," Sloane said. "I know the country."

"I'd better ride alone," Quaid said. "Excuse me. I have to see Wardell."

He turned and walked away, knowing he had been rude and that Lynn would be angry with him, but an ugly possibility had entered his mind when Sloane offered to ride with him in the morning. Maybe he was a Henderson man. If he was, he would probably see to it that Dan Quaid never reached Egan Creek alive.

Chapter 4

THE STREET DOOR of the C. and E. O. Land Company was open when Quaid reached it. The heat from the late afternoon sun was stirred but not cooled by the slight breeze. The instant Quaid stepped into the room, Wardell rose from his desk and demanded, "Well, did you see them?"

"I saw them," Quaid said. "You could have told me all they did and probably more. Why did you send me on a wild goose chase?"

"It wasn't a wild goose chase," Wardell said. "I wanted you to hear it from someone else. Besides, I wanted you to find out for yourself the kind of a son of a bitch Tobe Henderson is. Did you?"

A small grin tugged at the corners of Quaid's mouth. "I found out all right. I guess I'm supposed to be scared, but I'd like to know what kind of men the company sold to before. Did they back off when they saw what it was like?"

"I didn't sell to them, so I don't know," Wardell answered, "but I do have an opinion about you. I think you're stubborn enough to stay and fight if it kills you. Don't go up there with the notion you're headed for a Sunday School picnic."

The grin on Quaid's face widened. "I don't have any such notion. I expect it to be tough.

Maybe that's what appeals to me. Maybe I've never really figured out why I'm making this move. I didn't give you a very good answer this afternoon."

"No, you didn't," Wardell agreed, "but I thought I'd get it sooner or later."

"You're going to get it now," Quaid said. "I just couldn't stand the Willamette Valley any more. My good years were getting behind me without me finding out how good a man I am. I'm going to buy that land, Wardell, if it's all you say it is, and find out how good I am. If I ain't a better man than Tobe Henderson, I don't deserve to make the grade."

Wardell nodded as if he understood. He asked, "Did you ever kill a man?"

Quaid was taken back by the question. "No," he said. "I never have."

"You will if you last, so you'd better make up your mind to it. It's reached that point. Tobe Henderson has killed or at least tried to." Wardell loosened the scarf which was tied around his neck and pointed to the red scar which made an ugly circle around his neck. "Henderson and his two oldest boys would have hung me last spring if Matt Runyan hadn't showed up and made them let me go. You've heard of Runyan?"

Quaid nodded, shocked by the rope burn on Wardell's neck. He had known with the conscious part of his mind that he would be in a tough fight if he moved to Egan Creek, but the brutality of which Henderson was capable was driven home to him in a way that it had not been before.

"You still want to look at that section?" Wardell asked.

"I sure do," Quaid said, "but I'm glad you showed me that. I guess I didn't really know what I was up against."

"You do now," Wardell said grimly as he tied the scarf again. "You see, I'm a sort of trouble shooter for the C. and E. O. The company had sent some incompetent men here. The townspeople had been alienated by the high and mighty attitude of my predecessors, so my first job was to mend some fences. I think I did a pretty good job. Men like Rufe Langer and Billy Mason are fair-minded. I had to prove to them that the company is just as interested in the welfare and prosperity of the county as they are. I think you'll get more attention from the sheriff's office than our previous buyers did."

"Not if I'm dead," Quaid said.

"Your first job is to stay alive," Wardell admitted, "but you can count on the company giving you all the help it can to keep you alive. Well, I started to tell you what happened to me. I went up there in May hoping to make a deal with men like Tobe Henderson and Orrie Bean and the rest. There are nine families squatting on company land in Egan Valley. I was instructed to contact them and either pay for their improvements, or to let them buy the land at a reasonable figure.

"I never got a chance to talk turkey. Henderson and two of his boys heard who I was and what I was there for. They jumped me where I was camped and started to string me up. They'd have killed me if Runyan hadn't showed up. He's a queer one, but he has more influence up there than anyone else, and he balks at murder. So they let me go and I came back to town and I haven't been up there since."

"What did Mason do?"

"He arrested Henderson and his two boys. Ten men came down from Egan Creek and swore that the three Hendersons were playing poker all that night in Orrie Bean's saloon, so Mason turned them loose."

"The hell," Quaid said.

"That's how it is," Wardell told him. "Didn't Mason explain how it was?"

"Yeah, I guess he did," Quaid admitted. "I just didn't believe it."

"You'd better believe it," Wardell said. "That was the trouble with the other agents the company sent here. They thought the old West had disappeared by 1890 when the government said the frontier was gone. I'll admit that Egan Creek is the only place where we've had trouble, but what my predecessors should have known is that the West has always spawned a certain amount of lawlessness and violence. There are islands of it left all over the West and they'll be here for a long time."

"I've got one question," Quaid said. "Why don't you evict people like the Hendersons?"

"It's a natural question," Wardell said. "That's exactly what we will do if we have to. It may come to that if you fail, but there are several reasons why we are reluctant to solve the problem that way. In the first place, there is a good deal of sympathy with the squatters all over Central Oregon. You see, Tobe's father, old Gabe Henderson, was one of the first and most respected settlers in the county. Folks know what Tobe is, but most of them will tell you that he has good and sufficient reason for doing what he does. There would be some killings if Mason takes a posse up there and uses force. That would throw public opinion against us. My instructions are to keep it on our side."

"It will be on Henderson's side regardless of what happens to me," Quaid said.

"No, I don't think so. The law is on your side. If there is violence and a killing or two, it will be Henderson's fault. Everybody in town knows that. I mean, whatever feeling there is against the company does not apply to you."

Quaid nodded, thinking that was probably true.

"There are a couple more reasons. One is that

there was unquestioned fraud years ago when the wagon road was built. Or not built, as old Gabe and Matt Runyan contended. When they were fighting in the courts, there was a great reservoir of ill will built up against the road company because a number of settlers, and old Gabe was one, honestly thought they were settling on Government land, only to find out that they were squatters and could not prove up on what they thought was a proper homestead."

"I don't blame them," Quaid said.

"No, you sure can't," Wardell agreed, "but now it's over with. The trouble is the C. and E. O. inherited that ill will. The third point is that this is the day of the muck rakers when the rights of the common man are being held up to public view in national magazines and the big corporations are every man's villains. We have a lot of land to sell to a lot of John Smiths. We can't afford that kind of publicity, so we're gambling on you. We've got to win the bet. You'll be fighting for us as well as yourself."

"You haven't scared me out," Quaid said, "if that's what you're trying to do."

Wardell laughed. "No, it wasn't. I suppose you've figured out by now that you're our handpicked man. All I've been trying to do is to make sure you understand the risk." He walked to his desk and took a piece of paper from one of the drawers. "Here is a map of Egan Valley. I don't think you'll have any trouble finding your section. It lies two or three miles up Egan Creek from the town of Egan which isn't much of a town, just a schoolhouse and Orrie Bean's store and saloon. He has some rooms for transients over the store, but don't take one of them. You'll be safer camping by yourself somewhere."

Quaid shoved the paper into his pocket. "I'll start in the morning. I suppose I'll be gone about three days."

"Or more. Don't hurry, Quaid. This is the biggest move you ever made. You can't afford a mistake. Neither can we. You won't really fight unless you're convinced that section of land is where you want to live the rest of your life. When you get up there, don't tell anybody what you're doing there."

"Tobe Henderson and his boy know."

"Maybe they won't see you. You won't have any trouble riding around their spread. It's the T Bar just above town. Now I have one more suggestion. You'd better take a man with you and not run the chance of being lynched that I did. I can recommend . . ."

"No, I'll ride alone," Quaid said. "I'll see you when I get back."

He left the office, his shadow a long, dark streak on the dust beside him. It was time for supper and he was hungry. If Johnny wasn't back from the livery stable, he'd find him.

His thoughts turned to Sam Wardell and he wondered with a sudden burst of resentment why the man had said as much as he had, even wanting to send a bodyguard with him. Dan Quaid had been wiping his own nose for a long time and he could do it in Egan Valley, Tobe Henderson or no Tobe Henderson.

Chapter 5

PETE SLOANE sat beside Lynn in the lobby of the hotel, his gaze on Sam Wardell's office across the street. He was vaguely aware of Lynn's chatter although he didn't have much idea what she was talking about. Then a great silence suddenly descended upon them. He glanced at her, wondering what had happened. She had folded her hands on her lap and was glaring at him, her cheeks red with rising anger.

"Yeah, it sure is a purty country," he said.

Lynn dipped her tongue in acid and said slowly, "Pete Sloane, I hate you. You weren't listening to a word I said."

He bowed his head in shame. "I am guilty, your highness." He got down on his knees beside her, his hands laced together and held up in a plea for mercy. "Before you send me to the chopping block, will you give me a chance to explain?"

She laughed in spite of herself. "Get up, you fool. Go ahead and explain until you're black in the face, but it won't do you any good."

The lobby was empty except for the clerk who was watching in silent amusement. Pete sat down in his chair again and pointed a forefinger at the clerk. "Don't pay no attention to her, Slim. She loves me. She just ain't discovered it yet."

"Love you," Lynn cried out, shocked. "Why, you maniac, I just met you this afternoon. If your friend the clerk hadn't introduced us, I'd . . ."

"Ah, but that is the point," Pete said. "You see, Slim caught the message you sent him when you saw me at dinner. He knew you fell in love with me the minute you saw me, so he introduced us and I took you riding. It is true that I am poor of purse, but I am honest and my heart is pure. . . ."

"Oh, shut up. You're such a fool." She giggled. "I guess you're the craziest man I ever met."

"I'm sure I am," Pete said. "Now about my misconduct. I am abjectly sorry for it and I apologize in the most groveling manner. You see, I am poor in purse like I just said. I've been hanging around town looking for work, but I ain't found a thing. Now your dad is going to need a man and I need work, so it seemed sort of natural-like for us to get together."

"He's kind of stubborn," Lynn said doubtfully. "He cut you off pretty short a while ago. I don't think he'll hire you." She remembered she was supposed to be angry, and added tartly, "Besides, this has nothing to do with you not listening to me."

"Oh, but it has, dear lady," he broke in. "Your dad's yonder in Sam Wardell's office and I've been watching to see when he comes out. When he does, you put in a word for me."

"It won't do any good even if I wanted to," she

said firmly. "You know what he said about riding with him. . . ."

"Listen." He reached out and took her hand, his flippant manner leaving him. "You folks are new, but I've been in this country for a long time and I've worked in Egan Valley. I know those people. The trip he's making tomorrow is dangerous, too dangerous for one man. For his own good he ought to take me with him."

Her eyes widened. She whispered, "Pete, are you really serious for once?"

"I was never more serious in my life," he said. "Your dad don't know it, but he needs me tomorrow more'n he ever needed anybody in his life."

She jerked her hand from his, saying softly, "Here he comes."

Pete rose, hoping that Quaid had not seen him holding Lynn's hand. He had a hunch that the big man did not approve of his taking Lynn riding this afternoon. Maybe he was jealous of any man who paid attention to the girl. If that was the case, Quaid was in for a hard time because pretty girls were in demand in this country and Lynn was about the prettiest girl Pete had ever seen.

Then Pete saw his fears were groundless. Quaid was still in the street. Pete said, "Remember now. You speak up for me."

"I tell you it won't do any good," the girl said.

"You can wind him around your little finger," Pete said.

"Sometimes," she agreed, "and then there are other times when nobody, not even Mamma, can change his mind."

Quaid came in. He scowled when he saw Pete and Lynn standing on the other side of the room. He slowed up, then shrugged his broad shoulders and turned toward the stairs. Pete nudged her with an elbow and she called, "Pa."

He turned to them. Lynn said, "We want to talk to you a minute."

He walked toward them. "Where's your mother?"

"In her room," Lynn answered. "Asleep."

"Johnny?"

"He's still at the stable, I guess," Lynn said. "I haven't seen him come in."

"Time for supper," Quaid said. "I'll get him. You wake your mother up. Now what is it you wanted to talk about?"

"Pete says the trip you're making tomorrow is real dangerous and you ought to take him along with you," Lynn said.

"It's a little more'n that, Mr. Quaid," Pete added. "I'm out of a job and you're going to need a man. . . ."

"I don't figure on hiring anybody," Quaid said sharply, "and I told you a while ago I was riding to Egan Valley alone."

"But Pa, if it's as dangerous as Pete says . . ."

"What he didn't tell you is that it might be more dangerous having him with me than if I was alone," Quaid interrupted. "Now you go wake your mother up."

Wheeling, Quaid strode out of the lobby. Pete stared at his back, deciding that Lynn had made an understatement when she'd said he was kind of stubborn. He murmured, "I guess this was one of the times when nobody could change his mind."

"It certainly was," Lynn said angrily. "I get so mad at him. Maybe you'd better let Ma talk to him. She might . . ."

"No, let it go," Pete said. "Well, you've got to wake your ma up and I've got to dig up some supper. Thanks for your company this afternoon."

"Thank you," she said smiling. "We'll be here a few days. If you're . . ."

"I'll be busy till Saturday night," he said. "There's a dance in the Oddfellows Hall. If I get back in time, maybe you'd go with me."

"I'd love to," she said cuttingly, "if I'm still here and if I'm not busy and if some other man hasn't asked me to go with him."

He touched the brim of his hat and grinned at her. "That's fair enough," he said. "If I do get back and if I get cleaned up in time and if they ain't played 'Good Night, Ladies,' I'll see if you can go."

"You are crazy," she said and couldn't keep

from laughing. "Sometimes I wonder if you're ever serious."

"I was plumb serious about working for your dad," Pete said. "So long."

He left the lobby, wondering what Quaid had meant about it being more dangerous if he was with him than if Quaid was alone. Maybe he thought Pete was an assassin hired by the Egan Valley bunch. The idea made him laugh, but it wouldn't be laughable to Quaid.

Pete had supper in a restaurant at the end of the block, thinking it was a good idea to stay away from the hotel dining room. He didn't want to see Quaid again tonight. He drifted into the Stockmen's Bar and asked if anyone had seen Ike Tilden, a rancher from the other side of Grizzly Butte, remarking that he'd heard Ike was hiring. He had a drink, sat in on a poker game, and when it was dark, he dropped out, saying he'd have a look around town for Tilden.

He ambled along Main Street as if looking for the rancher, then rounded the corner and walked rapidly to Sam Wardell's house. He circled so that he came into the alley and stood at the corner of the barn on the back of the Wardell lot. He whistled twice and waited.

Mrs. Wardell was still puttering around the kitchen. Pete could see her bobbing back and forth as she put things away. Presently the back door opened and Wardell stood there filling his pipe and tamping the tobacco down. He yawned and said, "Guess I'll step outside for a little fresh air."

"Take your pipe with you," his wife said. "I declare, Sam, I don't see how you can stand that thing. It's strong enough to walk by itself."

Wardell laughed. "It must have taken a walk. I had a hell of a time finding it tonight."

"I hid it," she said, "but all you had to do was to follow your nose and you'd come right to it."

"That's just what I did," he said.

He struck a match on the wall and held the flame to the tobacco. When the pipe was drawing well, he stepped off the porch and walked slowly toward the alley until he was clear of the circle of light from the house, then he hurried across the back yard to the barn, saying softly, "Where are you, Pete?"

"Here," Pete said, and drew back along the side of the barn.

Wardell joined him asking, "Did you get a chance to talk to Quaid?"

"Yeah. It worked out fine. His daughter's the prettiest filly you ever seen. I got lucky and took her riding. She introduced me to her pa and I said something about riding with him tomorrow and he cut me off at the pockets. I was still talking to the girl when he left your office and I got her on my side, but it wasn't no use. He acts like he thinks I'm an Egan Valley man."

Wardell laughed shortly. "Maybe he does. I

tried to work it from my end, but he wouldn't have any part of it."

"He's stubborner than a square-headed Swede," Pete said. "What do you think of him?"

"He'll fight," Wardell said. "I put him through everything I could think of. I sent him to see Henderson and the boy before they left town, then he talked to Mason and Langer. After he came to see me, I shoveled on some more. The higher I piled it, the more he wanted the land. I don't think he'll quit, but he may be into a fight before he's ready for it."

"He'll get a fight," Pete said. "You can count on it. Well, I'll light out and camp on the river and wait for him to go by. It ain't gonna be easy, though. He's about the most independent bastard I ever seen."

"That part's all right if he doesn't overdo it. I guess you know what to do."

"What I do depends on what Henderson does," Pete said. "Where's Henry Oglethorpe Dawson?"

"Don't call him that," Wardell said. "It makes him mad."

Pete laughed. "I like to make him mad."

"I don't know," Wardell said. "He left town with his peddler's rig about a week ago, so he's up there somewhere. Chances are you'll find him along the river. He was heading for Egan Valley first and then was going to drop back along the river somewhere."

"I'll watch for him," Pete said.

"Good luck."

"I was born lucky," Pete said, and stepped into the darkness of the alley.

He got his horse from the livery stable, telling the hostler he hadn't seen Ike Tilden and he guessed he'd ride out to Grizzly Butte. If he didn't get a job pretty soon he'd have to quit eating. He took the road that led downriver, then when he was out of Prineville, he swung back and hit the upriver road half a mile above town. By the time the half moon was up in the eastern sky, he had found the camp site he had in mind.

Later, with his head on his saddle, he wondered how long Dan Quaid would last and whether he'd do the company's dirty work the way Wardell was hoping he would. He was a good man to bet on. He might make it, Pete thought. He just might make it.

Chapter 6

QUAID reached the junction of Egan Creek and Crooked River late in the afternoon. The distance had been greater than he had thought, so he was later getting here than he expected. Now he was tired. He had ridden steadily since dawn, dismounting only a few times during the day to stretch. He rubbed his buttocks and the inside of his thighs each time he was on the ground, for he was not used to riding so many hours at a stretch.

He thought ruefully that he had lost something since he had left the John Day where he had ridden all day, week and after week, without thinking anything about it. The farming years in the Willamette Valley had softened him for ranch work. Whatever he had lost must be regained if he was to become a cattleman, and that, he told himself, was exactly the reason he was here.

He dismounted and loosened the cinch and watered the bay. The gelding was the best Quaid had been able to find in any of the Prineville livery stables and was adequate for this trip. Buying a good string of horses for ranch work was something else. He'd heard of an outfit up the Ochoco that was supposed to have good stock. He'd take a look as soon as he got back to Prineville and finished the deal with Wardell.

Then he thought with wry amusement that there was no doubt in his mind about buying the company's land unless it was far below Wardell's description.

He glanced down the road and saw a horseman swing around a bend in the river. He frowned, irritated by this because he had suspected for several hours he was being followed. The rider had made his appearance sometime in mid-morning and had kept just about this distance between him and Quaid all day.

Quaid wasn't sure it meant anything. The horseman was never close enough for Quaid to recognize or even know whether he had seen the man before or not. Several times he had disappeared and Quaid would decide he had turned off to one of the ranches he had passed, but within an hour or so the rider would show up again. He could, of course, be an Egan Valley man who had spent the night in town, or he might be bound for the Burns country on beyond the head of Crooked River.

Still a sense of uneasiness nagged at Quaid. Tobe Henderson knew who he was and what he was planning, and Henderson might very well have paid someone in Prineville to tail him. Even so, the rider might not intend any harm. There had been plenty of lonely places where he could have shot Quaid if that had been his intention.

Quaid walked around for a time, trying to work

the stiffness out of his legs. He was near enough to the end of the day's ride to know he could go the rest of the way. He tightened the cinch and, stepping into the saddle, turned left through a narrow gap in the rimrock. The road followed the creek, climbing rapidly for the next mile or so, the stream pounding over the rocks to his right in a series of falls.

He came to the level floor of the valley quite suddenly, topping the last steep pitch to see it spread out before him. The effect was startling. The valley was a sort of bowl surrounded by rimrock so that the first glance made a man think there was no way out except through the narrow channel cut by the creek. As he rode on toward the cluster of buildings which would be the settlement of Egan, he saw there were occasional breaks in the rimrock by which a horse and rider could reach the plateau above the valley.

Quaid had been told there were fifteen ranches here. He counted almost that many before he reached Egan. Most of them were along the creek. The bottom land which could easily be put under a ditch was about a mile wide and made a solid belt of green, running above the town. A few ranches lay back from the road near the base of the rim, probably where some stockmen had found a spring breaking through the ground.

On both sides of the meadows the land sloped gradually toward the rimrock. Here was the finest carpet of bunch grass Quaid had ever seen. He judged from what he'd heard that the valley had been settled for a good many years and most of the sagebrush had been grubbed out, but there were patches here and there tall enough to hide a man on a horse, and that, he knew, was a sign of fertile land.

As he approached Egan he saw that the north end of the valley lifted in a series of pine-covered hills. From these hills timbered ridges knifed down into the valley. The section of land he aimed to buy would lie above the settlement and stretch on into the lower hills.

Somewhere beyond the company land would be Matt Runyan's home. He was the one man in this country in whom Quaid was interested. He would try to see him before he left. From what Wardell had said, Runyan was not an unreasonable man. If Quaid could make friends with him, he would cut trouble down to a size he could handle.

The meadow land was fenced. Now, just short of the settlement, Quaid saw a sign beside a gate, T BAR, TOBE HENDERSON, OWNER. A lane angled through the bunch grass toward a group of ranch buildings which were set near the base of the rim. The center of the house was made of stone and was two stories high. The log wings on both sides had probably been added later. Beyond the house were the bunkhouse, cookshack, barns and other outbuildings.

All of it, along with the corrals, gave an impression of permanence and efficiency. Here was unquestionably a ranch of great value, although why any man, Tobe Henderson or his father Gabe, would invest so much money in a ranch which by law did not belong to him was beyond Quaid's understanding. He knew nothing about old Gabe, but Tobe was certainly no fool.

There was something here Quaid did not understand. He thought about it as he swung out of the saddle in front of Orrie Bean's store and tied the bay. Apparently this was a situation which had gone on for a long time. It seemed only logical for the company to come to some kind of an agreement with Henderson. Obviously any fair price for his improvements would be high.

If this had been the Henderson home for thirty or forty years it was understandable that he would not want to sell his improvements and move on, so the natural settlement would be for Henderson to buy the land from the company. But perhaps he was too stubborn to pay anything, or again the company, aware of the value of the land that the Hendersons had developed into a fine ranch, had demanded a high price. In effect, this was asking Henderson to pay for value which existed only because of his own sweat and labor.

Quaid shrugged and turned toward the store. The cause of the stalemate, whatever it was, had nothing to do with him buying company land. One thing was sure, he told himself. He wouldn't spend a nickel to improve the section he planned to buy until he had a deed to it.

Two horses with T Bar brands were tied at the hitch pole. Quaid was not carrying a revolver, but he did have a .30-30 in the scabbard. For a moment he considered taking the rifle with him and then dismissed the thought. If he had to fight two Hendersons with his fists, he'd do it, but certainly there was no reason for any shooting.

The store building was a sprawling log one with two doors, one opening into a saloon, the other into the store. There was a second storey which was probably cut up into the rooms Orrie Bean rented to transients. On beyond was a log house that likely was the home of Orrie Bean and his family. Across the road was the schoolhouse, the only frame building in the settlement. Egan, as Sam Wardell had said, was not much of a town.

Quaid stepped into the store part of the building, the air feeling cool after the harsh sunlight. He heard the murmur of talk from the saloon. Then a man stepped through the connecting door and stood staring at Quaid, his dark eyes wicked with hostility. He was an older man than Quaid, probably in his fifties, big and slow moving.

"You're Orrie Bean?" Quaid asked.

The storekeeper gave a bare half-inch nod and remained silent, his dark eyes never leaving

Quaid's face. Quaid said, "I'd like some grub. Cheese, crackers, a couple cans of peaches, some coffee and bacon."

"I'm out of all of 'em," Bean said.

Quaid's first reaction was one of sharp anger. He knew Bean was lying and considered saying so. He even thought of going back to his horse and getting his rifle and forcing Bean to sell him the grub he wanted, then decided against it. He had not brought any food with him, a mistake he shouldn't have made. He'd have his look at the land this evening and start back in the morning. Once he was out of the valley, he could get a meal at one of the ranches he had passed earlier in the day.

He started toward the door when he heard a man say, "Hey, Rusty, it's the feller with the web feet."

He wheeled. Two young men had come through the door from the saloon, one as long-legged and gangling as his son Johnny. He was a little older, probably nineteen or twenty. The second was clearly a Henderson, as stocky and knot-muscled as Tobe Henderson and the son Quaid had seen in Prineville. Whether this one was younger or older than the boy who had been with his father was a question. In either case there wasn't more than a year's difference. They could even be twins.

The stocky one had his revolver in his hand.

His meaty lips thinned against his teeth in a taunting grin. He said, "You know, Rusty, it rains so much on the other side of the mountains that fellers like this one get webs between their toes and they waddle like a duck. They've got moss on their backs, too."

"I don't believe it," the slender boy said. "I don't think he's got webs between his toes, either."

"Sure he has," the stocky one said. "Now let's see. The moss would be on the west side, wouldn't it? That's the direction the rain comes from, ain't it?"

"I reckon it is, but you're crazy, Bronc. He ain't got a west side. He's bound to turn around once in a while. When he does, the west side will be his east side."

"Naw, they get so they can't turn. It's so wet that they grow roots right out of between the webs. That holds 'em down, solid."

"Sure, that's the way it is," Quaid said, thinking this was just good-natured hoorawing and he'd better take it as such. "We get so we have our backs to the west all the time."

He started toward the door again and stopped two steps from it. A bullet splintered the casing, the sound of the explosion hammering against Quaid's ears.

"Stand right there, mister," the stocky one said. "Rusty here don't believe you've got any moss on your back. I aim to show him you do. Now pull off your shirt."

"Better do it, friend," Orrie Bean said. "This here is Bronc Henderson and he's almost as ornery as his pa."

Quaid turned slowly, so angry he was trembling. It was incredible that anyone, even a Henderson, would kill a man for not taking off his shirt, and yet, looking at his smirking face, Quaid knew that was exactly what Bronc Henderson would do. This was no good-natured hoorawing. It was murder.

Chapter 7

HENRY OGLETHORPE DAWSON wore many hats. He had worked for the Cascade and Eastern Oregon Land Company for several years in various capacities. This was the first time he had ever been in Egan Valley. Since he wasn't known in the valley, he wore the hat of a peddler. He had spent five days there, visiting every family and selling a variety of articles from needles and thread and pins to flavoring, perfume, liniments that were good for man or beast, and cough syrup that was designed strictly for adults.

He had rented a room from Orrie Bean, telling him blandly that he was stealing some of Bean's business, so he thought it was only fair that Orrie get some of it back for room rent and the whisky that Dawson drank in Orrie's saloon. Actually the arrangement did not work to Orrie's benefit because there was a poker game going every night and Dawson left the valley with about fifty dollars of the storekeeper's money which did not help Orrie's disposition or dull his wife's tongue.

Dawson was a lawyer, an expert appraiser of property, and the kind of man who could meet other people at their level; qualifications which made him ideal for the job the company had given him. He was to gauge the temper of the Egan Valley families who were squatting on company land and at the same time place a value on the improvements each family had made.

Wardell had come to the valley in the spring, making no secret of who he was or why he had come, and had nearly been lynched by the Hendersons without having a chance to talk to them or any of his neighbors. That was why the company had sent Dawson to work out of Prineville. As a peddler Dawson could go to the valley, meet the squatters, and leave without creating a disturbance.

Now Dawson was camped on Crooked River below its junction with Egan Creek. He didn't know the day Dan Quaid would arrive in Prineville, but Wardell had given him the approximate date and had ordered Dawson to watch for him. If he didn't show up or got scared and pulled out of the deal, Pete Sloane would be along to tell him. Sloane might be along anyhow, Wardell had said, if it looked as if Quaid would need help.

So he had waited, and now his patience had run out. Inactivity had always galled him, and sitting in a camp beside the river for two days had almost been too much for him. He was a banty of a man with a scarred face and a blob of a nose and bright blue eyes that could be filled with merriment one moment and be as hard and glittering as two matched diamonds the next.

He had permitted his red beard to grow for this occasion. It was now at the proper length to stand straight out all over his face so that he resembled a grizzled porcupine.

Dawson had no idea what Dan Quaid looked like. He scrutinized each rider carefully who went past his camp. When Quaid finally did ride by late in the afternoon, Dawson guessed his identity, partly because of the new Stetson, and partly because his face lacked the dark bronze that it would have had if he'd been a native. A few minutes later Pete Sloane turned in from the road and Dawson knew his guess had been a good one.

"About time you were getting here," Dawson said. "I've been waiting for two days and I'm not a waiting kind of man."

Sloane grinned as he dismounted. "So the great Henry Oglethorpe Dawson ain't long on waiting."

"Don't call me that, damn it. I've told you a thousand times. . . ."

"I know," Sloane said, "but I've seen the door of your office in San Francisco and it has Henry Oglethorpe Dawson on it in big black letters which also say he will take any and all law cases if there's enough excitement and risk to 'em."

"You lie as easy as a horse trots," Dawson grumbled. "Anyhow, in this country I'm Hank Dawson, peddler. You'd better remember it."

"I'll try, Mr. Attorney, I'll try," Sloane said. "How was business in Egan Valley?"

"Good, considering. I've got a report for Sam." Dawson shook his head. "But that's the damnedest country. They act as if they're living in the 1880's and to hell with the law."

"Take the Hendersons out and they're not such bad people," Sloane said. "Sam knows that. If the other agents who had been sent to Prineville had had that much sense, we wouldn't be in this fix."

"And maybe you know how to deal with the Hendersons," Dawson said.

Sloane's quick grin touched his lips. "Well no, Hank, I don't. But Sam figures Quaid's our man. The way I see it, the company made two mistakes. One was in sending agents to Prineville who thought they were God Almighty, and the other was in selling to men who ran scared whenever Henderson made a face at 'em."

Dawson fished a short-stemmed pipe out of his pocket and filled and lighted it. He said thoughtfully, "I don't know about that, Pete. Sam's inclined to think he's God Almighty, too. Sure, he's the company's top agent and he's working at this slow and easy which is right, but if it hadn't been for Matt Runyan he'd be dead. I don't see how that makes Sam look real smart."

"He learned the hard way, all right," Sloane admitted.

"I know the men who own the company and

call the turn," Dawson said. "They sit in their fine offices behind mahogany desks and count their money and hire men like us to go out and take the risks. If we get killed, that's too bad. If we fail, we get fired, and if we succeed, we get paid but no thanks go with the pay."

Sloane rolled a cigarette, stooped and picked up a lighted twig from the fire and touched the flame to his cigarette. He said, "You're talking like a damned socialist, Hank. What kind of a capitalist is going to give thanks along with the pay?"

"I'm no socialist and don't you call me one," Dawson said hotly, "but this whole deal stinks to high heaven. They don't want a lot of unfavorable publicity which they'd get if Billy Mason goes up there and uses force to evict the squatters. The company's about to start an all-out campaign to sell the company land in Central Oregon because a railroad is coming up the Deschutes and Prineville will probably get a spur. We might even get one up Crooked River."

"Nothing wrong with that," Sloane said.

"No, except that we're the ones who have to figure out how to handle a tough bastard like Tobe Henderson. I played poker a couple of nights with him. The best place in the world to size up a man is over a poker table. I tell you, Pete, that son of a bitch is the meanest, toughest, most stubborn booger this side of hell. He'll kill our man Quaid and Quaid's blood will be on our hands and on Sam's."

"You must have lost some money to Henderson," Sloane said.

"A little," Dawson admitted, "but I came out ahead, mostly at Orrie Bean's expense. I spent about half a day on the T Bar and sold Mrs. Henderson some stuff and talked to the boys. The youngest one, Rusty, is a good kid, but Shep and Bronc are just like Tobe. The old man didn't show up while I was there, so I was glad to see him come into Bean's and sit in on the game. When he didn't have the cards, he folded. When he did have them, he'd go all the way. No bluffing. No finesse. Just power. When he sets out to win a pot, he never backs up, never turns a corner."

"That's Tobe," Sloane said. "I worked for him during spring roundup. All the time I wondered what would happen to me if he ever suspicioned I was a company man."

"I had the same question in my head when I was playing poker," Dawson admitted. "Well, what kind of a fellow is Quaid?"

"He's all right," Sloane said. "Big and stubborn as all hell. Independent, too. I tried to work it so I'd come up here with him, but he wouldn't stand for it." He glanced at the sun. "Hank, if you can think of an excuse, maybe you ought to ride up to Bean's place. Quaid didn't bring no grub which was a mistake, but I couldn't give him any advice, and he'd have got suspicious if Sam had tried."

"Has Quaid got any family?"

"A wife, a son about 17 or 18, and a purty daughter who's about a year older."

Dawson knocked his pipe out and dropped it into his pocket. "Quaid's a pawn," he said angrily. "Just a pawn and the company doesn't give a good God damn about what happens to him."

"What do you mean by that?" Sloane demanded. "We're trying to keep him alive, ain't we?"

"And he's the one who's risking his neck, isn't he? And why? Because if he sticks, others will follow and buy company land. The company's got a hell of a lot of good ranch country to sell, and if conditions were different, it could sell it."

"Quaid knows he's risking his neck," Sloane said. "Sam did everything he could to tell him how tough it is up here."

"You can tell him a hundred times," Dawson said. "He'll hear it with his ears and know it with the top of his head, but he won't really know. Not with his heart and guts until he's been through the mill. By that time it may be too late."

"Nobody's making him buy the land," Sloane said. "It's a damned fine section that the company is practically giving him."

"But he's still a pawn," Dawson said doggedly.

"What Sam really hopes is that Quaid will kill Tobe Henderson. If Quaid hangs for it, Sam will be sorry. That's all. Just sorry. Once Henderson is out of it, Sam can handle the others. I'll probably have to make the offers. If Henderson is dead, I can do it without running the chance of being shot to pieces. Was anybody honest enough to tell Quaid that?"

Sloane laughed. "Honest enough? Or crazy enough? You'd better take a sashay up there, Hank. I'll ride in after dark, but if I showed up now, it might turn the animals loose. Tobe thinks I'm a drifter. He'd sure be curious about why I'm back in the valley."

"All right," Dawson said. "I'll take your horse."

"Go ahead," Sloane said. "Just don't waste a lot of time on the way."

Dawson walked to his rig, pulled a .45 from a holster that was under the seat, and slipped the revolver under his waist band, the skirt of his corduroy coat dropping over it so it was hidden.

"I don't aim to tarry," he said. "If I do, you'd better hitch up and find out what happened to me."

He mounted and rode up the river. He had worked for the company in one capacity or another for a long time, and he had been associated with Sam Wardell and Pete Sloane for most of that time, but he had never before experienced the distaste for the job that he did now. He wasn't sure why he felt this way, but he did know that he would never forgive himself or the company if Dan Quaid was killed.

Chapter 8

THE ANGER that was in Dan Quaid as he faced Bronc Henderson grew into a wild and compelling fury he had never experienced before in his life. He saw anxiety in the eyes of the younger Henderson boy; he sensed that Orrie Bean was coolly indifferent to what Bronc Henderson did. There would be no help from either.

"Get that shirt off, mister," Bronc Henderson said. "I ain't gonna wait all day. Rusty wants to see the moss, and by God, I aim to see he gets a chance. Now get it off. You hear me?"

Quaid made his decision, as coldly logical as any he had ever made in his life. He had told Sam Wardell he wanted a challenge, wanted to find out how good a man he was. Here was the challenge. If he knuckled down and took off his shirt, the news would be all over the valley in a matter of hours. He would be a laughing stock; he would have no man's respect, and he would be whipped before he ever saw the land he planned to buy.

Maybe Bronc Henderson would shoot him, but there was a chance the boy was bluffing. It was a slim chance, but the only one Quaid had. He said, "Henderson, you'd better put that pistol back in the holster. If you don't, I'll take it away from you and I'll jam it down your throat."

He took a slow step toward Bronc, then another, his eyes never leaving the boy's face. Bronc backed up, yelling, "Stand pat, mister. You ain't taking no gun away from me."

"Hold it right there, both of you," a man said from the doorway. "Bronc, I'm surprised at you, getting yourself out on a limb on account of some transient who happens to drift into the valley."

Quaid wheeled toward the door. A little man stood there, a long-barreled .45 in his hand that looked almost as big as he was. He wore cowhide boots, khaki pants, a corduroy coat, and a peaked, stiff-brimmed hat. He had a bristly red beard that gave him a faintly comical look, but there was nothing comical about the hard expression in his blue eyes or the way he handled his gun.

"Stay out of this, Dawson," Bronc said. "It ain't none of your . . ."

"Maybe not, maybe so," Dawson said, "but I'll tell you one thing. I'm not standing still while you kill a man for nothing. I don't know who he is or what he's doing here, but I know what'll happen if you shoot him. Now you boys get on your horses and slope out of here."

"He's a mossback from the Willamette Valley," Bronc said hotly. "He's up here to look at company land he's aiming to buy. Pa won't stand for it."

"All right then," Dawson said. "Leave it up to your pa. He's supposed to be stubborn and ornery, but he's smart, too. The situation is damned touchy right now and you know it. All the company needs is for a man like this fellow to get killed and Billy Mason will be up here with a posse and the whole Henderson family will be evicted and you'll hang." He jerked his left hand at the horses and stepped away from the door. "Now git, both of you."

"I reckon he's right, Bronc," Orrie Bean said. "Let your pa handle it his way. He'll know what to do with this gent."

Bronc slowly lowered his gun and holstered it. He said sullenly, "Pa will handle it, all right. That's one thing you can be God damned sure of. Come on, Rusty."

They stalked out, Bronc in front, Rusty following two steps behind. Quaid watched until they mounted and rode toward the T Bar. Dawson holstered his gun as he said, "You were raising hell and propping it up with a chunk, friend. Were you trying to commit suicide?"

"It wasn't my idea," Quaid said. "I aim to buy land and live in this valley. What do you think would have happened to me if I'd got down on my knees in front of that kid?"

"You'd have kept on living," Dawson said. "That's what." He looked at Bean. "Orrie, you're a fool. This gent means nothing to me and neither does Tobe Henderson, but they should have meant something to you. This kind of killing would blow the lid off. You could have stopped Bronc."

"No need to if you hadn't showed up," Bean said callously. "Me'n Rusty would have swore it was self defense and nothing would have happened to Bronc."

"Doesn't a human life mean anything to you?"

Bean shrugged. "Some do, some don't," he said. "You were up here long enough to know the shape we're in."

"I sure do," Dawson said. "I told you then you couldn't go on living this way, making your own rules and acting as if Egan Valley was an independent republic. Matt Runyan's the only one up here with any sense. He'd better talk to you again."

"What'd you come back for?" Bean asked. "I thought you said you were heading down the river toward Prineville."

"I was, but I got to thinking that I'd gone off and forgotten to pay you for the room. You remember whether I did or not?"

Bean blinked as if he considered this a strange reason to bring a man back to Egan Valley. He said, "You paid."

"I wanted to be sure before I left the country," Dawson said. "The laws are pretty tough on a man who doesn't pay his hotel bill and I didn't want you to get the sheriff after me."

He turned and walked to his horse. Quaid caught up with him and held out his hand. "I'm Dan Quaid," he said. "Thanks for what you did just now."

Dawson shook hands with him. "My advice to you is to get the hell out of Egan Valley. You haven't got a chance up here. What Wardell didn't tell you is that the company is using you and it doesn't care what happens to you."

"I figured that," Quaid said, "but you see, in my own way I'm using the company."

"It's your choice," Dawson said sourly.

He mounted and rode away. Quaid sighed and, going to his horse, pulled the rifle from the scabbard and went back into the store. He said, "Bean, you're going to sell me the grub I asked for a while ago."

"Go to hell," Bean said.

Quaid cocked the rifle. "I've never killed a man, but I guess I will if I stay here. It's like Dawson asked you a while ago about whether a human life means anything to you and you said some do. Well, I'll tell you damned plain that yours don't mean nothing to me after you stood there and let the Henderson kid do what he done. I don't aim to go hungry while I'm here, so you get that grub put together."

"All right, all right," Bean said. "I ain't looking

for trouble, but you are, and I'd say your chance of finding it is good. Real good."

Fifteen minutes later Quaid left the store, his groceries in a gunny sack which he tied behind his saddle. He mounted and rode upstream, his gaze ranging from one side of the valley to the other. He could expect anything now, but he was reasonably sure that Tobe Henderson was not at home or he'd have made his appearance before this.

He saw only one small ranch upstream from the store. He studied the map again that Wardell had given him. Two miles above the store he would cross the section line and be on the land he planned to buy. The sun was almost down now. He would make a thorough study of the land in the morning. The light would soon fade, but he could see enough to know that Wardell had not exaggerated the possibilities of this place. All it would take was work. And peace, he thought angrily.

Wardell had said there was about 150 acres of bottom land that could easily be irrigated. Quaid estimated there was more. It was covered by bunch grass with very little sagebrush and only a few small junipers. Ahead of him the timber was a dark mass, making a wide half-circle on both sides of the stream. He glanced at the map again, then at the hills that lifted gradually from the creek bottom and guessed that the section corners would just about be on top of the hills on each side of him.

He dismounted when he reached the cabin and kicked at the dirt; good black loam that needed only to be turned and planted and watered. He saw very few rocks. The valley was far different from much of this country. There a man had to swing around one outcropping of rock after another and was constantly running a chance of breaking his plow on one that was hidden in the ground.

He opened the door and looked into the cabin. Dirty, of course, with no furniture except a bunk, a home-made table, and a stove, but it was tight. He could live here with Johnny until he knew it was safe to bring Angie and Lynn. Then he thought with a sense of guilt that he had never asked Johnny if he wanted to come. He had simply assumed that the boy would want to be with him.

If Quaid chose to risk his life for a piece of land, it was his business, but he had no right to put his son into the same danger. He should have considered Pete Sloane who wanted a job. Well, he'd find another man to work for him and he'd leave Johnny in Prineville. It would be fall or later before his family could come, maybe a long time later.

He left the cabin, again making a quick study of the open country around it that lifted toward the timber. All the Hendersons could be hiding up there in the pines, he thought, just waiting for a good shot. He grinned wryly. He guessed he was getting jumpy. Then he wondered about the man who had built this cabin and what had happened to him and to the others who had come here thinking they could stay and later found they couldn't.

As he walked toward his horse, he felt something round and hard under his foot. Glancing down, he kicked it out of the dirt. It was a doll head, faded almost beyond recognition. The body had rotted away. For a long moment he stood there staring at it, thinking it was symbolic of a tragedy, a family's dream that had ended so quickly and perhaps so painfully.

All the things Sam Wardell had said came back to him, and what Billy Mason and Rufe Langer had said, and the fellow named Dawson who had probably saved his life. He stepped into the saddle, knowing that in his way he was just as stubborn and perhaps foolish as Tobe Henderson. He could not back up, for now he had seen the land. If he rode off and left it, he would be haunted by his own failure as long as he lived.

He glanced downstream toward the Narrows through which he had ridden an hour or more ago; he saw the transient red of the sunset touch the upper edges of the rim, then the deep purple of the evening settled down upon the valley. He noticed how the long line of rimrock gradually broke off into the gentler, timber-covered slopes that bordered the upper valley. He smelled the pine scent and the sharper tang of sage, he felt the cool air of the mountain evening, he heard the whisper of wind and the rustle of the creek below him.

The scene was hauntingly familiar. He wondered if he had ever been here before and realized at once he had not. Could he have dreamed of it and then forgotten? He had an odd, compelling feeling that this was home and he had finally come back to it; he knew that no matter what the risk was, he would buy this section of land. He could not go off and leave it.

He rode upstream for a quarter of a mile and there among the first pines he staked out his horse and built a fire and cooked his supper. By the time he had finished, the twilight had become night. He threw more wood on the fire so that a tall, bright blaze lifted toward the sky. Then he slipped back into the darkness and sat down to wait for Tobe Henderson, his back against a small pine, his rifle in his hand.

Chapter 9

TIME DRAGGED painfully for Quaid as he waited. He was tired in every bone and nerve and muscle of his body. He had ridden more miles since he had left Prineville than on any other day in twenty years. His legs and buttocks were so sore it hurt him to move, but he couldn't risk having the fire burn out. He wanted a big blaze so that Tobe Henderson would have no trouble finding him. When the fire began to die down, he threw on more wood and quickly drew back into the darkness.

He was so worn out that occasionally he dropped off to sleep in spite of himself, but he would wake up at once when his head bobbed down to his chest. He gripped his rifle with both hands, his eyes probing the darkness beyond the fire as he wondered if some unusual noise had wakened him, a man-made noise that meant the Hendersons were coming. Then a few minutes later he would repeat the pattern.

For some reason which he did not understand the weariness began to leave him around midnight and he became alert, perhaps because he sensed that this was the time they were most likely to come. The mountain air was cold now;

it was as if the hot day of a few hours before had never been.

The fire made an island of light in front of him, the darkness surrounding and covering him. There was no moon in the sky. Overhead the starshine was a faint glow in the slopes of the heavens until it was blotted out by the black ridge lines on both sides of the valley. Now and then some small animal slithered through the dry leaves under the willows beside the creek and made a rustling sound. A night bird swooped toward him and lifted and was gone, the echoes of its call lingering for a brief time in the silence.

As he listened to the undertones of the night, a strange feeling possessed him, as if the wildness of the mountains had flowed down from the peaks to the north and had taken possession of his body. He had never felt this way in the Willamette Valley with its regular routine of seasons and work, the slow movements of their way of life, the reasonable certainty that he would be alive tomorrow and tomorrow and tomorrow.

He would not go back to western Oregon; he could not. Angie, he knew, would never share this feeling. He doubted that Lynn ever would, but Johnny might. Perhaps it was man feeling: the feeling that he had tried to explain to Sam Wardell and had not fully succeeded because it was something which could not be verbalized.

He heard a coyote call from somewhere above him on the ridge. It was an expression of the wildness that was in him, and because of that, he felt a sympathy with the animal. At this moment he thought he was very close to answering the questions that had always plagued him; questions that have plagued all men from the beginning of time. Then he heard the horse coming upgrade and the spell was broken.

He rose and stepped farther back into the darkness. He heard the sound of his own breathing, a raspy sawing of air as it entered and left his lungs. He wondered what the thumping sound was that he heard and then realized it was the beating of his heart. He laughed silently, some of the tension leaving him. It wasn't so much that he was afraid, he told himself. He simply recognized the importance of these few minutes. At least it was the end of the waiting.

A moment later Tobe Henderson rode into the circle of firelight and dismounted. He called, "Quaid! Show yourself. I know you're here. This fire didn't build itself."

Quaid hesitated. He hadn't expected Henderson to come alone, but none of his sons were in sight. He asked, "Where are your boys?"

"I don't know," Henderson said. "Why the hell should I? You think I was afraid to show up here by myself?"

Again Quaid hesitated, not liking this, but

deciding it would be like Henderson to come alone. Quaid watched him move toward the fire, leaving his rifle in the scabbard behind him. As far as Quaid could see, he was not carrying a gun. He stood there with the firelight dancing on his square, bronze face, his bold eyes probing the darkness.

Tobe Henderson was like a block of granite, Quaid thought. There was nothing pretty or nice about him. Sweat had stained his shirt under his armpits. He needed a shave. His clothes were worn and soiled. He stood with his thumbs slipped under his waistband, teetering back and forth on his heels, a tough and unyielding man who had made his own laws for years and had no intention of changing.

"Why are you here?" Quaid asked.

"I wouldn't be here if you had the sense of a curly-haired idiot," Henderson said angrily. "I told you in town how it was. If you come up here to settle on this land and tell the company to go to hell, you'll be our neighbor and we'll be glad to have you. But if you pay the God-damned company five cents an acre, we'll run you out of the country, if you're alive long enough to be able to run."

"You think I'd be as big a fool as you are?" Quaid demanded. "You think I'd make the kind of improvements you have on land I didn't have title to?"

"You can call it being a fool," Henderson said, "but I know what's right and what's wrong. It's right for us to live on our land and make our living from it, and it sure as hell ain't right for the company to own land it didn't do nothing to get. That's it in a nutshell. Now it's up to you. You going to be with us, or are you going to do business with a thieving, robbing company that says it's gonna run us out of our homes?"

"I don't doubt that you suffered an injustice," Quaid said, "but you aren't the first and you won't be the last. Sooner or later you'll be evicted. Why don't you make some kind of a deal with Wardell so you'll own your place?"

"We own it now," Henderson said. "My pappy, old Gabe Henderson, settled there before anybody ever heard of a wagon road grant or the Cascade and Eastern Oregon Land Company. He fought the Snakes. Had a brush with Chief Paulina right down the creek a piece and killed two of his bucks. I was just a baby then, but I've heard him tell it a hundred times. Our sweat and our blood has gone into this land. You think we're moving out and handing it over to a bunch of get-rich-quick bastards in San Francisco?"

"It's what you'll do in the end," Quaid said. "Right or wrong, you'd do what you have to do to save your ranch. I'm buying, Henderson. I'd be a fool to do anything else."

"Come on to the fire," Henderson said. "I'm

gonna beat hell out of you. I told you in town what would happen."

Quaid moved to the edge of the fire. He said, "I don't figure to take any beating, Henderson. I've got my Winchester. I'll give you ten seconds to climb into your saddle and git."

"Not me," Henderson said. "I came here to give you a beating and that's what you're gonna get."

Two of the Henderson boys dived out of the darkness and were on him before he knew they were there. Each gripped an arm with both hands and hustled him toward the fire. He was stunned at the first moment of impact, then he tried to lunge free. He twisted and kicked and yanked; his Winchester fell out of his hands when they first grabbed him, but he would not have had a chance to use the rifle even if he had kept his grip on it. One of his captors was the oldest boy, Shep, the other was the second son, Bronc, who had tried to kill him this afternoon. Each was as heavy and strong as he was. He was completely helpless against the two of them.

Henderson moved around the fire toward him. He said again, "I told you in town what would happen."

He swung a fist at Quaid who was still straining and twisting to free himself. The blow caught him in the belly, slamming breath out of him and sending a great wave of pain all through his body. He lunged out with both feet, swinging so that his entire weight was on the boys who held him, his boots catching Henderson in the crotch.

The big man bent over, groaning and motionless. Shep cursed as both boys jerked Quaid back so he couldn't kick Henderson again. Bronc slammed a down-swinging fist that caught Quaid at the base of the neck. His knees turned to rubber and he would have fallen if the boys hadn't held him upright.

Painfully Tobe Henderson straightened and moved in, his fists hammering Quaid on one side of the face and then the other, rocking his head back and forth as if it were a ball attached to a string.

"Kill him," Bronc said furiously. "What are you bunging your fists up for?"

Henderson straightened and rubbed his hands against his pants' legs. He saw blood trickle down Quaid's face from his nose and a smashed lip and cuts on his cheeks. He said, "No, we won't kill him. When he comes around, he'll change his mind about a few things."

Henderson put a hand under Quaid's chin and, lifting his head, studied his face. He withdrew his hand, letting Quaid's head sag. He said, "Let him go."

They released their grip on his arms and he fell full out on the ground and lay still. There was nothing but blessed blackness; Quaid had not felt the last blows.

Chapter 10

PETE SLOANE had supper ready when Hank Dawson returned. He watched the little man as he dismounted and took care of the saddle horse. Something had happened, but Sloane wasn't going to ask. He would let Dawson tell him in his own good time.

The truth was Sloane had been jealous of Dawson for years and he still was. Dawson could do many things and do them well. Masquerading as a peddler in Egan Valley was an example. Sloane would have bet a year's pay that no one in the valley had the slightest idea that Dawson was anything other than what he appeared to be.

If Dawson had been satisfied to stay in his office in San Francisco and work at being a lawyer, he would have done very well. He knew the law, and when he appeared before a jury he had a fiery eloquence that made a deep impression on anyone who heard him. But that was not the kind of life that appealed to him. He simply couldn't remain still. He loved activity too well. That was why he went to work for the company in the first place. Now he was in the field most of the time where he had enough activity to keep him interested, but where his knowledge of law was of great value, too.

For several years he had been the company's top trouble shooter and its highest paid field man. The pay was one reason Sloane was jealous; the other was that he always felt inferior around Dawson because he could play no part except the role he was playing now, that of the good-natured cowboy, the drifter who worked here and there and could listen without appearing to listen and then report back to the agent.

Sloane did have one other talent. He was very good with either a rifle or a revolver and he had no compunction about killing a man if the killing was necessary and safe for the company. This was the only rule that Sam Wardell laid down. In a showdown, the company would never admit that Pete Sloane worked for them. If he got into trouble, he was on his own. That had been made plain to him in the beginning.

Not that the company condoned murder. If Wardell and Sloane conspired to kill a man who stood in the company's way, they were responsible and Sloane would answer to the law. All the company required of any of its men was that its policy work. It was up to Wardell and Sloane to decide what would make it work.

Resentfully Sloane thought about this as he watched Dawson come to the fire and help himself to coffee, bacon, and biscuits. He had never been sure how much of a conscience the lawyer had. He did know that more than once

Wardell had not taken Sloane into his confidence when he had told the full truth to Dawson. This was one of the things that added to Sloane's anger, particularly when he considered the risks that each of them took for the company.

"You've eaten?" Dawson asked.

Sloane nodded. "I wasn't sure when you'd be back."

Dawson nodded. "No, I guess you weren't. You'd better light out for the valley. Quaid's going to need you before morning unless I'm mistaken."

Sloane reached for tobacco and paper. "That so?" he said with feigned indifference.

"It is if I read the sign right." Dawson told him what had happened in Orrie Bean's store, and added, "I can't understand that damn fool Bronc unless he's been in Shep's shadow all this time and he just had to do something big. I don't savvy Orrie Bean, either. He knows what Matt Runyan says."

"Maybe Orrie's tired of walking slow and easy," Sloane said. "People get that way after a while. I do."

Dawson looked at him intently. "What do you mean by that?"

"I mean I could go into the valley and watch my chance and drill Tobe Henderson right through the brisket and get out without anybody knowing who did it or why it was done. What's more, nobody in the valley would give a damn except Henderson's own boys."

Dawson was shocked and showed it. He said, "I know the men who run the company. I know them a hell of a lot better than you do and maybe better than Sam does. They'll do almost anything to make a profit on their investments, anything but murder."

Sloane shrugged. "That's what Sam says, but the point is that we've played this careful for a long time. We can't go on playing it careful if the company is going to sell its land in Egan Valley by the time the railroad gets to Bend."

"I know that," Dawson said angrily. "That's what makes me so mad. We've all been told the company won't condone murder, but it will condone selling the land to Dan Quaid who has more guts than brains. Sam knows that if Quaid kills Henderson, the company has won the fight and still has its skirts clean. If one of the Hendersons kills Quaid, it will probably work the same way, especially if someone like me is on hand to see the killing. Sam could put enough pressure on the sheriff to get results. Whoever killed Quaid would hang because I don't think Runyan will stand for murder."

"And that means the Hendersons wouldn't have a lot of witnesses swearing they were all playing poker when it happened."

"It looks to me as if it's just another way of

chasing the rabbit around the bush," Sloane said. "I might as well do the job myself."

"But you might get the company involved and there'd be hell to pay," Dawson said. "As far as the end result is concerned, it's the same. Quaid deserves better treatment. He trusts Wardell. Even after I told him the company was using him. . . ."

"You what?" Sloane shouted. "Why, you God-damned fool, that's the last thing Wardell wanted him told."

"I know it," Dawson said coldly. "That's why I told him. I've got my belly full of Wardell's tactics. I'm going to tell him that when I get back to town. What's more, I'm going to speak my piece to the Prineville newspaper. These are decent people up here in the valley. Most of them anyway. They deserve a better deal than Wardell will ever offer them."

"Henry Oglethorpe Dawson, the crusader," Sloane said softly. He was pleased. He had never heard this kind of talk from the lawyer before. It was, he thought, the end of Dawson's job with the company. He added maliciously, "Sure sounds like you got religion."

"I finally did, but it's been a long time coming," Dawson said bitterly. "I guess what really got under my skin was when I told Quaid the company was using him, but he just kind of grinned and said in a way he was using the company. He's a lamb going to slaughter. He doesn't know Tobe Henderson, and if you don't get up there, he's in for a hell of a beating."

"Yeah, guess I'd better."

Sloane rolled and lighted a cigarette, turning this revelation over in his mind. And it was a revelation. Dawson had such a good arrangement with the company that it had never occurred to Sloane that the lawyer would rebel at what he was asked to do or at what he saw being done. He was a fiery kind of man who never backed off from a job because it was hard or dangerous. Perhaps Dawson did know the men who sat behind their mahogany desks and ran the company, but Sloane knew Sam Wardell.

"Get moving," Dawson said impatiently. "I'm worried about Quaid. He's a hell of a good man."

"I was just thinking about you," Sloane said. "We've worked together for a long time and I always figured we were good friends, so I'll tell you something. Sam Wardell is a tough son of a bitch. He knows what he's got to do. He knows it's got to be done right, and he knows time is running out on him."

"What are you trying to say?" Dawson demanded.

"I'll make it real plain," Sloane said, "since you need it plain. If you tell him you're quitting and you're telling what you know to the newspapers, he'll shoot you right between the eyes."

Dawson laughed and motioned toward the horse. "Get along," he said. "I don't know why you're trying to scare me unless it's because of some misbegotten sense of loyalty to the company. But if I know anything at all, I know Sam Wardell isn't a killer. He'd tell *you* to do it if he was worried about what I was going to tell, but *he* wouldn't."

"All right," Sloane said. "I've warned you."

Later, as Sloane was riding through the Narrows, he laughed when he thought about it. Dawson was smart in most ways, but he had a contrary streak. Sloane didn't doubt that Dawson would do exactly what he had said he would and that Wardell would shoot him. At this stage of the game, Wardell simply couldn't afford to let Dawson run loose with a wagging tongue. With Dawson out of the way, maybe Pete Sloane would be a little more valuable to the company.

After Sloane passed Orrie Bean's store, he swung east away from the creek, riding slowly and pausing often to listen. It was dark now and he didn't want to run into the Hendersons. He had no intention of looking out for Dan Quaid and he grinned when he thought about Dawson's concern for the settler. Sloane couldn't imagine why any company man would be that concerned about Quaid.

Presently he saw Quaid's fire through the scattered pines, a big fire that would certainly draw Tobe Henderson to it long before morning. Dan Quaid was a fool, Sloane told himself contemptuously. Or else he was far too confident of his ability to handle the Hendersons, and that made him a fool.

Sloane kept riding until he was on the ridge above Quaid's fire, then he dismounted and tied his horse and settled down to wait. He wanted a cigarette, but he couldn't risk one. He almost fell asleep once and had to get up and walk around to jar himself. Why didn't they come and get it over with?

He glanced often at the stars trying to judge the hour, and had the frustrating feeling that time was standing still. Later, sometime after midnight, he heard a horse on the road downstream from Quaid's fire. He had watched Quaid throw wood on the fire several times and dart back quickly into the darkness, so apparently he was expecting the Hendersons, but what he didn't know was that some of them had silently worked their way through the timber between Sloane and Quaid's fire. At least he was reasonably certain that was what had happened. He hadn't seen them, but he had heard a faint sound of movement on the slope below him and now and then the snapping of a dry twig. Besides, it was what he had expected the Hendersons to do and what Quaid should have expected.

He saw Tobe Henderson appear in the firelight,

and although he could not see Quaid, he was certain from the way Henderson acted that the two of them were talking. Then it happened exactly as he thought it would. Two of the Henderson boys surprised Quaid. They were mountain men used to hunting deer and moving as silently as forest animals, so it had been no great trick to sneak up behind Quaid without warning him of their presence.

He watched Quaid take a beating, then saw the Hendersons leave Quaid lying unconscious by the fire. Sloane waited several minutes until the last sound of the Henderson horses had faded, then he mounted and rode down the hill to the fire. Quaid hadn't stirred. For a moment Sloane thought he was dead, but when he felt his pulse, he found it strong. Presently Quaid groaned. He'd be coming around soon.

Sloane, squatting beside the fire, considered killing Quaid. He could take a club and beat his skull in and even the Hendersons might wonder if they had been responsible for his death. He decided against it. He judged Quaid exactly as Dawson had. The man had more guts than sense. He wasn't likely to overlook this beating. When he was on his feet, he'd go after Tobe Henderson and that was exactly what Sam Wardell had wanted him to do all the time.

He filled Quaid's hat with water and sloshed him in the face. They'd done a job, Sloane thought, a typical Henderson job, the same job that had worked time after time and had kept people from staying on this section of land. But Quaid was made of different stuff. Wardell had picked his man with great skill.

Several minutes passed before Quaid was fully conscious. He sat up and dropped flat again, holding his head. Sloane said, "They sure worked you over, Mr. Quaid. They must have used a club on you."

"Fists," Quaid muttered through bruised lips. "Just fists."

"We've got to get out of here," Sloane said. "I know a cave on the other side of the creek. I'll take you there and you'll be safe until you're able to ride. There's a spring close to it and you can build a fire if you get back into the cave apiece."

"You think they'll come back?" Quaid asked.

"Sure they will," Sloane said. "I'm surprised they didn't use a rope on you like they done Sam Wardell. If they find you here tomorrow that's what they'll do."

Quaid tried to sit up again but the pain was still too great. He said, "I can't make it yet. Give me a little more time." He crawled away from the fire to a pine and sat up and put his back against it. He held his head in his hands as pain beat at him in agonizing waves. Sloane watched him in silent amusement.

"How'd you happen to show up here?" Quaid asked finally.

"I figured you'd need help," Sloane said, "so I followed you. I stayed back a piece 'cause I knowed you'd give me hell if I caught up with you. I still need the job, Mr. Quaid, and I think you'll give me one now. They'd have killed you tonight if I hadn't come along."

"You mean you ran them off?" Quaid asked.

"That's it. I surprised 'em. I told 'em I was working for you. I guess they was so busy pounding on you they didn't hear me come up. They were too smart to buck a man holding a gun on 'em, so they vamoosed. That's why I figure we'd better move as soon as you're able to ride. Now how about the job?"

"You're hired," Quaid said. "And thanks. I guess I needed help more'n I knew."

"It's all right, Mr. Quaid," Sloane said. "I was glad I got here in time. The point is any man can make a mistake, but he sure as hell can't afford to keep making 'em. It's just that I knowed these men and you didn't. You figure you'll quit?"

"No," Quaid said. "I won't quit. If you'll fetch my horse and help me into the saddle, maybe I can hang on long enough to get to that cave."

"Sure," Sloane said. "I'll fetch him."

He disappeared into the darkness, whistling tunelessly. He was running a risk that the Hendersons might discover them in the cave, but he thought the odds were ten to one against it. He was never a man to turn down a gamble if the percentage was right. On the whole it was working slicker than goose grease. It looked to him as if Tobe Henderson had about 24 hours to live. Quaid would need that much time to get over the beating enough to shoot straight.

Chapter 11

DAN QUAID rode bent forward, one hand clutching the horn, every jolting step his horse took sending a needle of agony through his head that felt as if it would rip off the top of his skull. But he hung on, across the creek and up the opposite slope until they reached the top. There Sloane stopped for the horses to blow. For a moment Quaid thought he was going to faint. He swayed in the saddle, the night-shrouded world wheeling in front of him, but he didn't lose consciousness.

Presently he asked, "How much farther?"

"A mile or so." Sloane was silent for a time, then he said, "We'd better git along."

After that it was a little better. They angled away from the rim, leaving the pines and threading their way through jutting lava upthrusts with here and there a few gnarled junipers. Presently Sloane said, "Here it is. Take it easy."

Sloane led the way down a steep trail that seemed to drop into the earth itself. Within a few seconds Quaid felt the cold slap of air from the interior of the cave. When they reached the bottom, Sloane said, "We'll stop here. No use going back into the cave. Fact is, I don't know how far it goes, but it must be a mile or two. It gets rougher'n hell and keeps dropping. Chances are we'd break a horse's leg and there sure ain't no sense in that."

Quaid dismounted and held to the horn for a time. He was surprised that at this point the floor of the cave was covered by sand. He backed up, feeling for the wall with his hands. When he found it, he sat down, knowing that if he didn't, he would fall down.

He put his head back against the smooth rock and closed his eyes. At this moment Tobe Henderson and the Cascade and Eastern Oregon Land Company and the wonderful section of land back there on the creek seemed far away and not very important. For some reason he thought of Angie's dream: "We made the move and bought the section of land on Egan Creek . . . nothing but trouble and suffering . . . and death."

He'd already had the trouble and suffering, and he had come close to death. Sloane said he'd saved his life. Maybe he had. Quaid hadn't really thought Tobe Henderson was a murderer, but he had almost murdered Sam Wardell. If Sloane was right, Henderson would have murdered Dan Quaid tonight. So maybe Angie's dream wasn't far wrong.

After Sloane took care of the horses, he brought Quaid's saddle to him. He said, "You'd better stretch out, Mr. Quaid. Put your head on the saddle and I'll throw these blankets over you. It's colder'n hell in here. I'll go up on top and scrounge around for some wood. There used to be a dead juniper close to the trail."

The rest of the night was a weird, nightmarish experience for Quaid. He'd sleep a few minutes at a time, then he'd wake up and see Sloane sitting by the fire, and he'd drop off again. If he remained absolutely motionless, his head didn't hurt much, but when he stirred in his sleep, it was probably the pain that woke him. He dreamed of being held by the Henderson boys and feeling their father's mauling fists, and that woke him again.

Just before dawn he fell asleep more soundly. When he woke the next time, warm sunlight was falling upon him through the mouth of the cave overhead. Sloane was gone and the fire had burned down. He got to his feet and swayed until he reached out and put a palm of his hand against the cold wall of the cave. Presently the dizziness passed. He walked slowly to the fire. Sloane had made a pot of coffee and the ashes were still hot. He set the pot in the ashes and squatted beside it wondering where Sloane had gone.

When the coffee was hot, he filled a tin cup and drank greedily. He put the tips of his fingers to his face and felt his battered nose and bruised lips and the scabs on his cheeks where Henderson's fists had broken the skin. He poured another cup of coffee and drank it more slowly, his mind turning again to Tobe Henderson.

The more he thought about the man, the more it seemed to him that Henderson's stand was impossible. Only a stupid man would believe he could go on holding land which by law he did not own, to continue running people off land which did not belong to him. Maybe he was stupid, Quaid decided. He and his father had suffered. Add that to the fact he was, by nature, a very stubborn man and the result was probably stupidity.

But there was a chance Henderson was running a bluff, a chance that no one had fought back. If Quaid did fight, Henderson might fold. Wishful thinking, perhaps, but it was a possibility worth exploring.

Sloane came down the steep trail carrying a canteen of water and an armload of wood. He said, "How do you feel, Mr. Quaid?"

"Fair," Quaid said. "Just fair."

"How's your shooting eye?"

"It will be pretty good when I get a little more rest," Quaid said. "I took a hell of a beating and I guess it's just going to take time."

Sloane built up the fire, glancing occasionally at Quaid. Then he said, "If you want to ride back to town and duck the Hendersons, we can stay here till night and then angle southwest till we hit the river."

"I don't aim to go back just yet." Quaid studied him a moment, then he asked, "How do you happen to know this country as well as you do? Take this cave. You came right to it."

"Why, I spent some time in Egan Valley," Sloane said. "Maybe I didn't tell you, but I worked for Henderson last spring. I know that bastard, Mr. Quaid. That was the reason I was so sure you'd need help, and it was why I followed you."

He poked at the flames for a time, and then added grimly, "The truth is he fired me, Mr. Quaid. Maybe I don't amount to a damn. I never claimed to be nothing great. I just drift around, working wherever I can, but I know what's right and what's wrong. Tobe Henderson gave me a hell of a bad deal, so I've got my own little debt to pay him."

"That why you wanted to work for me?"

Sloane nodded. "If you stay, you're into a fight, and I'd like to help lick that son of a bitch. Well, guess I'd better cook up a bait of breakfast."

Quaid returned to his saddle and lay down again. He felt better after he'd eaten. He found that he could eat without being dizzy and the pain in his head had subsided to a dull ache. He stared through the cave opening at the blue sky. The air from the interior of the cave kept its biting chill.

Later when he returned to the fire, he said, "This is a funny kind of a cave. I never saw one like it."

"There's a lot of them in this country," Sloane said. "Matt Runyan knows about these things and he says this is lava country. One of the most recent eruptions in the U. S. is here, he claims. Seems that a crust formed over the top of what he calls a lava flow and this was a kind of channel down here where we are. Later on, after it cooled off, the crust broke through where it was real thin. That gives us an opening into the old channel."

"The Hendersons know it's here?"

"Sure. We're close to the valley. Ride about half a mile due east and you'll come to the rim. You can look right down on Tobe's ranch buildings. That what you figure on doing, maybe warming him up a little? I'd like that."

Quaid filled his pipe. "I'm thinking about it. Henderson is counting on me crawling off and forgetting the whole thing. He's wrong."

Sloane nodded as if pleased. "I figured you were that kind of a huckleberry. Well, I'll go along with you and we'll shoot hell out of that house of his. He's gonna be the most surprised hairpin in Crook County. He's been a great one to dish it out, so it's gonna be fun to see how he likes the other end of the stick."

"No," Quaid said. "You're not staying here and

neither am I. If they found us, we'd be trapped and I'm not going to let that happen again. I want you to go to town and tell Sam Wardell I'll buy the property. Tell my wife I'm all right and that you're working for us. Then you go to the sheriff and tell him what happened."

"Billy Mason won't do nothing," Sloane said. "For one thing the company ain't real popular hereabouts and Mason likes the votes that come in from Egan Valley which same he got the last election. Another thing is he knows he couldn't prove nothing if he did arrest Tobe."

"I know," Quaid said. "I want him to know just the same. I don't aim to kill anybody, but I might, and I think I have reason to."

"All right, I'll tell 'em," Sloane said, "but I ought'a stay with you. It'll be the end of the line if they catch you again."

"They won't," he said. "Now go fetch my horse. I think I can hang on a little better than I did last night."

Sloane shrugged, "You're the boss."

Half an hour later Quaid was in the saddle and climbing out of the cave, Sloane following. When they reached the top, Quaid saw that the plateau around the cave entrance was a sandy desert covered with sage and rabbit brush and a few junipers. The Blue Mountains lifted above the plateau to the north. The scene to the south was that of a broken country, with rim after rim showing against the sky until the earth and the heavens met in the far distance.

Sloane pointed east. "You ride over that ridge yonder and you'll see Egan Valley. Keep going and you'll be right over Henderson's T Bar."

"All right, that's exactly where I'm going," Quaid said.

"When will you be in town?"

"I don't know."

"You want me to come back? If you do, I'll have to know where to look for you."

"I'll come to town."

"I'm going to have to tell your wife something."

"Just tell her I'll be there as soon as I can. And tell Sam Wardell not to sell that section of land to anybody else."

"He won't," Sloane said. "I'll bet on it."

Sloane nodded and, reining around, rode west. Quaid watched him for a time, wondering if Lynn was the real source of his interest. He rode up the ridge, thinking that it was just as well Lynn wasn't ready to settle down. Pete Sloane wasn't the kind of man he wanted Lynn to marry.

Quaid didn't have anything against a drifting cowboy, but there was something about Sloane he couldn't put his finger on. He'd have it if the man worked for him very long. Then he put Sloane out of his mind and thought about the Hendersons. He wasn't sure what he would do.

He wouldn't be sure until he reached the rim and studied the layout below him, but he was certain of one thing. As Sloane had said, Henderson was a great one to dish it out. Now it was Dan Quaid's turn to do the dishing.

Chapter 12

FOR THE FIRST TIME since he could remember, Hank Dawson could not sleep. Finally, with the first gray light of dawn seeping across the sky, he threw off his blanket and built a fire. He dipped water from the river into his coffee pot, poured coffee into the pot, and set it on the fire.

He washed his face and sat down beside the fire while the world slowly came to life around him. Little animals rustled through the dry leaves on the other side of his rig. He heard the whirring of wings as a bird took to the air from the tall green grass beside the river. From the hay field on the other side of the stream a meadow lark made the air sweet with its morning song.

The sky filled with color and presently the first sharp rays of the sun broke across the timbered ridge to the east and caught the ragged edge of the rimrock on the south side of the valley. Dawson glimpsed a coyote slither through the sage brush at the base of the rimrock and disappear. A buck came down to the stream and drank, then lifted his head as if catching a smell that worried him, and, apparently satisfied, drank again. From a ranch downriver a man let out a great yell for no logical reason unless it came from the mere joy of being alive.

Dawson drank a cup of coffee, then cooked his breakfast, and cleaned up his dishes. By that time he had made up his mind. He told himself he had never made a more important decision in his life and he wasn't exactly sure why he had made it. Usually his thought processes were as clear and cogent as any man's, but not this morning.

The truth was he could not get Dan Quaid out of his mind. He had a sharp mental picture of the big man starting to walk toward Bronc Henderson who had a gun in his hand, of Bronc who had got in over his head probably without intending to and would very likely have shot Quaid if the settler had kept moving toward him. Quaid was no fool. He must have known the risk he was taking.

If Quaid had run or if he had obeyed Bronc's crazy order to take his shirt off, he would have been a whipped man. He might just as well have stepped, into the saddle and ridden out of the valley. He knew that. Perhaps he was just as stubborn as Tobe Henderson, perhaps he could not back up or change directions any more than Henderson could. Or it might be that Quaid was driven by some force within him to see this land and buy it, a force so powerful that he took the very slim chance of staring Bronc down rather than admit defeat.

Whatever the reason was, Dan Quaid deserved a chance at the land he wanted and Dawson had decided to see that he got it. Having made that decision, he cursed his own stupidity for sending Pete Sloane into the valley to look out for Quaid. Dawson knew he should have gone himself because Sloane would use Quaid exactly as Sam Wardell in his scheming way intended for him to be used. Now the best Dawson could do was to return to the valley and do what he could for Quaid.

Dawson harnessed up and drove back through the narrows into Egan Valley, his revolver in its holster on his right thigh, the Winchester on the seat beside him. He did not expect trouble yet, but if Quaid was still alive and did not leave the valley, there would be trouble.

He passed Orrie Bean's store, noting that no horses were racked in front. He glanced to his left toward the T Bar but he could see no activity there. The Hendersons were early risers and probably were out on the range now. When he reached Quaid's camp of the night before, he was puzzled.

Dawson stepped out of his rig and slowly circled the gray pile of dead ashes as he studied the ground. There had certainly been a struggle. He found a few brown spots he thought were dried blood which might mean Quaid was dead or simply that there had been a hard fight and someone, very likely Quaid, had been marked up.

A moment later he discovered the tracks of horses and followed them to where they crossed the creek. If the animals were Quaid's and Sloane's, Quaid must still be alive, but Dawson wasn't satisfied. If Sloane was looking out for Quaid now, it only meant that Sloane was hoping to use him later on.

Dawson returned to his rig and drove on up the creek. Matt Runyan was the one man who might solve this entire problem. Now Dawson wished he had told the truth when he had seen the man a week before. At the time he was pretending to be only an itinerant peddler. When he thought about what the truth might do, he was frightened. If Runyan talked to Tobe Henderson, Henderson would hunt Dawson down and kill him if he found him. This, in Dawson's opinion, was a certainty.

Beyond the north edge of the company's belt of land the road climbed sharply through the yellow pines, the creek to his left. In places it had dug a narrow channel fifty feet deep, in other places it ran between gently sloping banks; but always it was hurrying as if it could not wait to reach the valley where it would be put to use to irrigate the land. Sometime before noon Dawson reached the level bench that held Matt Runyan's cabin. It was not large, but it was tightly built and neat with a few log outbuildings and a corral behind it. He had cleared a small piece of land on which he raised hay for his horses and had a garden of hardy vegetables which would grow at this altitude.

He was a strange man, and to Dawson, a very interesting one. He would have to be strange to be able to live apart from the rest of the valley people who were his friends. He was interesting because he read a great deal, putting all of his spare money into books, and because he was a kind of mystic who had a reputation for knowing things that he logically had no way of knowing.

Dawson stopped and tied the lines around the brake handle and stepped down. He heard Runyan chopping wood on the other side of the cabin, but the dog announced him before he saw Runyan. The animal had a most uncertain pedigree and looked like nothing Dawson had ever seen outside of his most horrible nightmares. He had short legs and a long body and ears that came to a sharp cock when something attracted his attention. He was brown and white and had long hair and a tremendous tail that thumped the ground whenever anyone paid the slightest attention to him.

The dog's name was Louis XVI. Runyan explained that he had named him that when he was a pup because he certainly was going to be decapitated if he didn't quit tangling with skunks. Then Runyan grinned and said he guessed the name hadn't really worked out. The dog was ten years old, he had not quit tangling with skunks, and he still had his head.

The dog came bounding around the cabin, barking a great welcome. Dawson stopped and petted him, the huge tail stirring the dust as it thumped joyfully. Dawson went on around the cabin. Runyan glanced up from his chopping block, evidently expecting some of the valley people, but when he saw who it was, he stood motionless for a full ten seconds, the axe raised in his right hand.

"Well, this is an unexpected pleasure, Mr. Dawson." Runyan lowered the axe and leaned the handle against the chopping block, then moved to meet Dawson, his hand extended. "I understood you were heading back to Prineville. After all, I bought everything I could from you this trip."

"I'm not here to sell you anything," Dawson said. "I'm here to talk and get some help from you if you'll give it."

"I have never refused help to anyone," Runyan said.

He was a tall man who appeared much taller than he was because he was all hide and bone. His hair was white, but his face had the appearance of a young man, partly because the skin was tightly drawn over the bones and was without wrinkles except around his eyes, and partly because the eyes themselves were bright and sharp and piercing. He wore a long drooping mustache which gave him a melancholy appearance that belied the good humor of his eyes.

"You'd better listen to me before you make any promises," Dawson said.

"Man was created to help other men," Runyan said. "I cannot conceive of a request for help that I would refuse." He motioned toward the door of his cabin. "Let's go in. I just started a fire and put the coffee pot on. Have you had dinner?"

"No, but I don't want to impose. . . ."

"You won't impose," Runyan said. "I shot a buck a few days ago, the first fresh meat I've had for a while. We'll eat reasonably well."

Dawson followed Runyan into the cabin and sat down at the table while Runyan cut two thick steaks from a hind quarter and started to fry them. The cabin had only one room with a bed, a bureau, and a filled bookcase at one end. The table and chairs were in the middle of the room, and the stove and shelves filled with groceries and dishes and pots and pans were at the other end. Everything in the room was clean just as Runyan's body and clothes were clean.

When Dawson had been here before, Runyan had showed him a deep pool in the creek just above the cabin where he said he took a bath every morning when he first woke up. When Dawson asked if he did the same even when snow was on the ground, Runyan looked surprised. He said, "Of course. A man must bathe in winter the same as in summer."

For a time Dawson watched him, keeping his silence, for he knew what would happen when he told him what he had come to tell. Runyan warmed up a pan of biscuits and poured the coffee and brought the venison steaks to the table.

"You can talk while we eat," Runyan said. "It's not often that I have company for meals. I wish I had more,"

"I might as well give it to you in one quick blast, Mr. Runyan," Dawson said. "I'm not sure you can help, but you're the only man who might be able to. That's why I'm here."

Runyan's lips smiled under his woebegone mustache. "All right. One quick blast."

Dawson put his hands palm down on top of the table and leaned forward. "I'm not just a peddler as you and everyone in the valley think I am. I'm a San Francisco lawyer and I work for the Cascade and Eastern Oregon Land Company. My purpose in coming here was twofold. First, to talk to the squatters in the valley and determine their temper. Second, to make notes which I will hand to Sam Wardell who will use them to decide on a price for the improvements. He will make an offer to every squatter in the valley in the hopes we can arrive at a settlement of this stalemate."

Runyan's face turned pale. His eyes widened,

the good humor leaving them. He started to get up, sat back, and then did rise and take two steps toward the rifle on the wall by the front door.

"Pete Sloane, who worked for Henderson at one time, is also a company man," Dawson hurried on. "Although he is the eyes and ears of the company in much the same way I am, he is also a sort of hatchet man. You see, certain policies are set down and certain results expected, and therefore much is left in the hands of the local agents. You can see what can and does happen."

Slowly Runyan returned to the table and sat down. He said in a low tone, "For many years I have understood something that few people do. Non-violence is the only way that man can live in harmony with God, and yet, knowing that, just now I turned toward my rifle. The first impulse that came to me was to kill you where you sit." He rubbed a hand across his face. "Can any man remove the devil from his own soul?"

"You have, I think," Dawson said, "and I've just made a long step in that direction. That's why I'm here and it's why I want your help. Now that I've given you the quick blast, will it make some difference if I tell you I do not trust either Sam Wardell or Pete Sloane, that I'm going over Wardell's head to the company, and if I don't get results, I will resign?"

"I don't understand," Runyan said.

"You know about Dan Quaid?"

Runyan nodded. "Tobe Henderson rode up here the evening after he had met this man in town. He said Quaid was coming to look at the company's upper section on the creek."

"That's right." Dawson told him what had happened in the store the previous evening, then added, "This is where your help comes in. I don't want Quaid murdered. I don't think you do, either. But if I'm reading the sign right, Sloane and Wardell don't care if he's murdered or not. That will get Tobe Henderson into trouble he's never dreamed about. On the other hand, if Quaid murders Henderson, the way is open for the company to move in, evict the squatters without bloodshed, and sell the land. If that happens, I suspect your friends will receive very little for their improvements and my report will be thrown into the waste basket."

Runyan was eating slowly and listening. He said, "I know about the business in the store. Rusty Henderson has left home. He took his horse and came by here. He said he couldn't stand it any longer. I don't know what he's going to do, but he certainly hates his father and the things his father does."

"Where is he now?"

"He went to town. He'll get a job if he can."

"He's not much like his pa."

"Not at all. He's not even like his brothers, but he is much like his grandfather, old Gabe.

He has courage, but he has principles, too, and he lacks the brutality that seems to control Tobe. His mother died several years ago, worn out by Tobe's attention, I suspect. That's the real reason Rusty hates his father. The whippings he's received have added to it, of course." He looked up from his plate. "What do you want me to do?"

"Help me save Quaid's life. And Henderson's, although I don't give a damn about him. I just don't want Quaid to hang for his murder."

"How can we save him?"

"We'll have to find him first. You know the country. They say you're a fine tracker. I think we'll have time to run him down before dark. It may be too late if we wait."

"All right," Runyan said. "I'll help, not because of Quaid, but because it will keep my friends out of trouble. I'm not counting Tobe Henderson among my friends. Our paths have diverged."

"Good," Dawson said. "We're working for the same thing."

This was the best he could do, he thought, and he was satisfied.

Chapter 13

WHEN DAN QUAID saw the rim just ahead of him, he dismounted and tied his horse in a narrow gully. Drawing his Winchester from the scabbard, he walked slowly toward the rim, his gaze sweeping the open country around him. No one was in sight. He saw nothing alive except a buzzard wheeling in the sky to the west and a band of T Bar cattle grazing on a ridge north of him.

He dropped flat on his belly before he reached the rim and wormed his way forward. He stopped just before he reached the edge, noting with pleasure that he was directly above the T Bar buildings as Sloane had said he would be.

The entire valley stretched out before him, from his camp site of the night before and the pine-covered hills north of it on south past Orrie Bean's store and the T Bar and the other ranches to the high rims that blocked in the valley on the south. From here he could not see the slim gap that was the Narrows. The road seemed simply to disappear into those high cliffs.

He studied the buildings below him. No smoke rose from the big stone chimney. He could not see any motion except among the horses in one of the corrals. He was close enough to hear sounds, but he heard no voices, nothing except the crowing of a rooster in the back yard.

He had thought about shooting out the windows of the house, but that would be only an act of vandalism with nothing gained, unless the Hendersons were there. The only thing he expected to gain was to scare them, at least show them he wasn't going to take a beating and not strike back.

All the Hendersons, even Tobe, were human enough to be scared. The fact that Tobe had not tackled Quaid until his two boys held him seemed to prove that. It took no great courage to beat up a man who was helpless. And in the store yesterday afternoon Quaid had certainly seen fear in the eyes of young Rusty Henderson. His brother Bronc had backed up when Quaid had started toward him. He'd held a gun and he might have shot down an unarmed man, but he had been afraid, too. It was the only way Quaid could account for his hesitation.

There was nothing to do but wait. He drew back from the rim and closed his eyes and dropped off to sleep, the hot sun on his back. At first when he woke he was aware only of aches and pains and stiffness. He felt completely drained, as if every muscle in his body had been torn loose from the bones to which they were anchored.

He rubbed his eyes, unable at the moment to remember why he was here and what he planned to do. Then it came back, and some of the weariness left him, and he thought, *I would never have dreamed of getting into this kind of a jam when I lived in the Willamette Valley.* He would have smiled if his lips had not been so swollen. He was a far different man from the one who had come to Prineville a few days before.

As he crawled back to the rim he noted that the sun was well down in the west. Peering over the edge, he saw Tobe Henderson standing beside a long trough near a corral gate talking to one of his boys who was watering his horse. Apparently he had just ridden in. At least his saddle was still on his horse. Another of the boys, he could not tell which was Shep and which was Bronc, came out of the barn and walked toward his father.

This was perfect, far better than he had expected the situation to be. He was an excellent shot with a Winchester, and at this distance he knew he could put a bullet exactly where he wanted it. He cocked the rifle and raised it to his shoulder just as Tobe turned toward the house. He squeezed off a shot, the bullet kicking up dust in front of the cowman. A second bullet lifted a small geyser of water from the tank, the third hit the ground in front of the boy who had just left the barn.

Quaid did laugh then regardless of the pain from his swollen lips. This was the funniest scene he had ever looked at in his life. For several seconds the Hendersons stood as if paralyzed. Perhaps they actually were, he thought. He guessed that nothing like this ever had happened to them before, so perhaps it was shock as well as fear that held them. They certainly heard the shots and saw where the bullets hit, but still it must have taken a little while for them to fully understand what was happening.

All three lifted their heads to stare at the rim, then they exploded into action at the same time. Tobe raced toward the house in lunging, awkward strides; the boy who had been watering his horse dived head first over the trough to the other side; and the one who had left the barn whirled and slipped and fell, and then, still on his hands and knees, he scurried crab-like toward the open barn door. The horse, boogered by the sound of the shots, had bucked across the yard and disappeared around the corner of the barn.

Quaid could not stop all three of them, moving at the same time as they did, so he concentrated on Tobe, laying his shots about halfway between Henderson and the back door of his house. He could have covered the area in which his bullets hit with his hat, each one stirring the dust of the dry yard.

Whirling, Henderson raced back toward the trough. He was neither quick nor graceful, and at the moment there was nothing tough or unyielding about him. He was just an ordinary frightened man trying desperately to reach cover.

Quaid stopped shooting to watch. Henderson's skin must be crawling, Quaid thought, for the man certainly was expecting the next bullet to rip into his flesh. He seemed to flounder, his legs moving under him, his feet slipping and sliding, his big arms pumping the air, and yet he was hardly moving. It probably seemed that way to him, too. Then he got traction and when he was still ten feet from the trough he threw out his hands and plunged forward, falling on his belly and sliding and scrambling to safety, dust whirling up around him. This time Quaid laughed aloud.

Quaid filled the magazine and waited. Presently the boy behind the trough poked his head up and Quaid fired, the bullet kicking up the water. The head promptly disappeared. Silence for several minutes then until the boy inside the barn called, "I've got him spotted, Pa. He's up there on the rim."

"Where the hell did you think he was?" Tobe yelled. "Up in the sky?"

"He's right above us," the boy shouted. "Above the chicken pen. I can see his hat."

"Knock it off his head," Henderson bellowed.

The boy emptied his revolver, none of the bullets coming close. He called, "It's too far, Pa. I ain't got my Winchester."

Again the silence ribboned out. It would soon be dusk, Quaid knew, the light too thin for accurate shooting. When that moment came, they'd saddle up, get their rifles, and come up here. They would have to ride upstream for some distance before they found a break in the rimrock, but it probably wouldn't be far. Just as well pull out now, Quaid decided. He would be asking for trouble if he stayed. He fired two shots into the trough to let them know it wasn't safe to show themselves, then he slid back and rose.

Quaid stopped, a long breath coming out of him as he thought how easy it would have been for one of the Hendersons to have come up behind him and shot him. Two men stood not more than twenty feet from him, but neither was the youngest Henderson boy. One was the red-bearded peddler who had bought into his trouble in the store; the other was a tall, old man with a sad-looking mustache. He had not seen the old man before and he wondered if it was Matt Runyan. There was a gentleness about him that Quaid had not sensed in any other man since he had arrived in Prineville.

"We were looking for you," Hank Dawson said. "We heard the shooting and decided it must be you. I want you to meet Matt Runyan."

The old man held out his hand. "I'm very happy to meet you, Mr. Quaid. You probably know that by now you are a marked man. At least you have ruffled the calm surface of the pool of life since you arrived."

"I've had my calm surface ruffled, too." Quaid pointed to the scabs on his face. "The Henderson boys held me last night and their dad beat hell out of me."

"That sounds like Tobe." Runyan nodded toward the rim. "What did you do to them?"

"Nothing except scare them," Quaid said. "At least I hope I did. I didn't hit any of them, but I could have killed all three. I had two pinned down behind a trough and one in the barn. I didn't see the fourth one."

"That'd be Rusty, the youngest one," Runyan said. "He never did fit the family pattern, so he left home."

"I'm sorry to interrupt," Dawson said, "but when they decide you've left the rim, they'll come barreling up here. We'd better be gone when they do. Where's your horse, Mr. Quaid?"

"In that gully," Quaid answered. "Where are we going and why were you looking for me?"

"It's a long story," Dawson said. "Too long to tell now, but we want you to go with us to Matt's ranch which is on up the creek a ways. I've got some salve that will help your face. Matt's a fair hand at doctoring, they tell me. After supper we've got some talking to do."

Quaid shook his head, suddenly wary. "I've got to leave here, all right, but I don't see any reason to go to Runyan's ranch. I aim to make life miserable for the Henderson tribe for a while."

"Where's Sloane?" Dawson asked.

"He's going to work for me," Quaid answered. "I sent him to town to let my family know I was all right."

"Well then, I'll tell you why you should go with us," Dawson said. "I'm not really a peddler. I work for the company. So does Sloane, but he takes his orders from Wardell who's trying to use you to pull the company's chestnuts out of the fire. His policy will lead to you killing Henderson or Henderson killing you. I aim to stop it. When I get to town, I'm wiring the company about what's going on here, but that's just half the fight. We've got to take care of the Hendersons, too. Scaring them with a few shots, or making life miserable for them as you put it, won't do the job. Maybe Matt here can figure out an answer."

"I think I can," Runyan said.

Quaid sighed. He had heard too much too fast, and it would take time to digest it. What Dawson had said about scaring the Hendersons with a few shots was right. He nodded, "I'll get my horse," he said.

A few minutes later they were riding north and had disappeared into the timber long before Tobe Henderson and his two sons reached the rim.

Chapter 14

WHEN RUSTY HENDERSON slipped out of the house and saddled his horse and left the T Bar in the middle of the night, he knew he was making a complete break with the old life. He would never come back; his father simply had no capacity for forgiveness. You were with him or you were against him. There was no middle ground. Now that Rusty had left, he knew he was going over to the other side. At least that was the way his father would see it.

Rusty had no regrets about leaving. If he had any regrets at all, it was because he had not left before. He remembered some happy times when he was very young and his grandfather had been alive. Old Gabe had been a fighter, but there was kindness in him too, a quality that seemed to have missed Rusty's father completely.

After his grandfather's death, his mother had gradually faded and had died four years ago. Rusty didn't know what had caused her death. It had seemed to him she had simply given up. His father, he thought, had been the reason.

She had found no pleasure in living, so death and the new life it had brought, whatever it was, must have been a relief.

Once, not long before she died, Rusty's mother

had called him to her. She had said, "There is more of life than what you have seen on the T Bar. You can find beauty and love if you look for it, but you will never find it here."

Now, thinking about what she had said, the thought occurred to him that she had been starved for love and beauty, and that great void must have hastened her death. She had not actually said he should leave home, but it was what she had meant. He had taken four years to find the courage to go, four years that had given him scars on his back from his father's blacksnake and scars on his face from his father's fists.

He didn't know where he would go or how he would live, but any life was better than the way he had been living. It was senseless to tell himself he should have left home when his mother died. The brutal truth was he could not have made his living when he was fifteen. Now, at nineteen, he could. He certainly owed nothing to his stepmother who was actually little more than a housekeeper as far as he was concerned. There was nothing to keep him from leaving home now. Nothing.

He stopped at Matt Runyan's at dawn. He would not have bothered the old man if he had been asleep, but he saw smoke rising from the chimney and he heard Runyan singing from somewhere about the cabin. Rusty tied his horse at the hitch rack and walked up the creek. Louis

XVI raced toward him, barking fiercely, and Rusty stopped to pet him. Then he saw Matt, completely naked, standing on the bank toweling himself briskly.

Rusty called, "Howdy Matt."

"Oh, it's you, Rusty," Matt said amiably. "I didn't know who it was, visiting at this hour. I'm glad to see you. As soon as I get my clothes on, we'll go get us some breakfast."

He dropped his towel and started to dress. Rusty went on until he was within two steps of the old man, then he stopped and decided he'd better tell Matt why he was here. His father and Matt had nothing in common except their hatred for the company, but Matt was so well liked by everyone else in the valley that Henderson at least pretended to follow his leadership. Now it might be different. Rusty guessed that his father would strike at anyone who befriended his traitorous son.

"Matt, I'd best tell you right out," Rusty said. "I'm leaving home. I don't know where I'm going or what I'll do, but I know I can't stay on the T Bar any longer."

Matt stuffed his shirttail into his pants and pulled his suspenders over his shoulders. "I'm not surprised one bit, son," Matt said. "How you've stood it this long is a mystery to me. Your family is kind of funny. Shep and Bronc favor your pa, but you favor your grandpa. I saw that when you were little. It was just like you were cut out of a different bolt of cloth. Well, come on and let's see what we can rustle for breakfast."

Rusty fell into step beside him. "Don't you understand, Matt? Pa don't give a damn about me except that I can do a man's work, and it takes four men to run the T Bar in slack times. Other times like roundup and haying he hires more, but he's always got to have four. With me gone, he'll have to hire another man."

"I expect he will. Hey, Louis," he yelled at the dog. "If you don't quit chasing that rooster, I'll take a stick to you. What's the matter with you?"

The squawking rooster disappeared inside the chicken house. The dog sat down and yawned, his tail thumping the ground. Rusty said, "Damn it, Matt, don't you understand? If Pa finds out I stopped here and you fed me, he'll raise hell with you."

"You mean I'd better be afraid of Tobe?" Matt shrugged, grinning a little. "Maybe I should. He's a rough one, but then again, maybe he should be afraid of me. He's outlived his day, Rusty. I guess I have, too, but I can change. The trouble with Tobe is he can't. It's just not in him, so he'll go on fighting everybody in the world. In the end it's going to kill him. I don't propose to let him take everybody in the valley with him. It's time he was told."

They went into the cabin, Matt leaving the front door open. The morning light was still very thin. He stoked up the fire and poured water and coffee into the pot and set it on the front of the stove. Rusty sat down at the table and stared at the old man, thinking that this was a kind of courage he had never seen before. His father could come up here and kill Matt with his fists. What was more, he was capable of doing it if he was cornered. Matt knew this, but apparently it didn't bother him at all.

Matt turned to look at the boy. He said, "You stopped here to get your backbone stiffened? Or was it advice you wanted? A loan? Or just breakfast?"

"No sir," Rusty said. "I guess I just wanted to talk. When anybody in the valley needs someone to talk to, they always come to you."

"I consider that a compliment," Matt said. "I aim to do all the things I just said. Maybe you don't need your backbone stiffened, but I suspect you do need the rest. I've got $50 I don't have any use for. You take it and pay it back after you get a job."

He sliced bacon and put the frying pan on the front of the stove, the pine snapping and cracking in the fire box. Then he turned to a shelf, took down a tin can and, removing the lid, counted out $50 in gold and gave it to Rusty.

"Money's the last thing I need," Matt said, "but

you'll need it where you're going. Now where is it you aim to go?"

Rusty stared at the gold and shook his head. "I was scared when I left home. I figured on going a long ways from here, maybe get me a job building the railroad on the Deschutes, but just now I changed my mind. I'm staying in Prineville. Maybe I can get a job. I'll stay there a while anyhow." He took a long breath, then he asked, "Is it wrong to hate Pa the way I do?"

"In the eyes of God it's wrong to hate anybody," Matt said gravely, "but it's a human thing to do. You have plenty of reason to hate him."

"I've got to fight him," Rusty said. "When he finds me, he'll try to take his blacksnake to me again like he's done plenty of times. He'll say I've got to work for him till I'm 21, but I won't do it. If it was just me'n him, it wouldn't be so bad, but I can't lick him and Shep and Bronc at the same time." He licked his lips. "But I was thinking that if I ran, I'd be a coward and I don't want Pa or anybody to think that."

"Seems that you don't need any advice and you sure don't need your backbone stiffened," Matt said, "so let's have breakfast. And no hurry about paying the money back. I know you'll do the best you can."

While they ate, Rusty told him about what had happened in Orrie Bean's store. Then he added, "If Dawson hadn't horned in on the show, Bronc

129

would have smoked Quaid down and I'd have been into trouble along with him. So would Orrie Bean."

Matt nodded. "That's the story of the valley, Rusty. It's why we've got to make it clear to everybody that it's time to change. We can't go on backing your pa any longer. We'll play right into the hands of the company if we do."

"I've thought about it ever since it happened," Rusty said miserably. "I don't know yet what was wrong with me, but I just didn't have enough guts to jump Bronc. I kept thinking about it after I got home and even after I went to bed. That's why I decided to pull out. If I'm going to fight my own kin, I'll do it in the open and everybody's going to know about it."

Matt nodded as if he understood the bitterness of self-condemnation that was in the boy. He said, "You can't go back and undo what's happened, but you can learn something from it so you won't do it again."

"I've learned it," Rusty said somberly.

He left a few minutes later, rode through the timbered peaks of the Blue Mountains to Ochoco Creek and followed it into Prineville. He left his horse in Barlow's livery stable, then he asked Barlow for a job.

"You're Tobe Henderson's youngest, ain't you?" Barlow asked.

"Yes."

"Don't he need you no more on the T Bar?"

"I didn't ask him," Rusty said. "I left home. Now I've got to have a job."

"Sorry," Barlow said. "I don't have nothing for you."

Rusty grabbed his arm. "Look, Mr. Barlow. I've been raised with horses. I can come as near to riding anything with hair on it as the next man."

Barlow jerked his arm free. "You think I'm crazy enough to do anything to get your pa down on me? He's always let me alone and I've let him alone and that's the way I aim to keep it."

He wheeled and strode off along the runway. Rusty stared after him, wondering if that was the reception he'd get everywhere he asked for a job. It was. By evening he had tried every place in town that might use a man and the answers were the same. Dejected, he went to the hotel in late afternoon and got a room. He'd stay a few days, he thought. Something might turn up. Maybe he could get a job on a ranch up the Ochoco or down the river.

He went upstairs, feeling so completely miserable that he wasn't looking where he was going. It stunned him to realize that his father's long arm reached from Egan Valley to Prineville without the slightest effort on the old man's part.

He was staring at the floor and bumped into the girl before he knew she was even in the hall. Apparently she had just darted out of her room.

She ran headlong into him and bounced off and almost fell. He grabbed her by the arm and steadied her. He blinked and dropped his hand from her arm, embarrassed. She was the prettiest girl he had ever seen, with dark eyes that were laughing at him and black hair and full red lips that seemed to be begging to be kissed.

"I'm sorry, ma'am." He snatched his hat from his head and knew he was blushing. "I guess I'm about the most awkward critter there is. I hope you ain't hurt."

"Of course not." Her laughter was gay and effortless. "It's my fault. My mother keeps telling me I'm too old to go bouncing around the way I do. If I'd come out of my room in a lady-like manner, it wouldn't have happened."

He started past her, then stopped when she said, "I don't remember seeing you here in the hotel before, Mr. . . . ."

"Henderson. Rusty Henderson." He paused, thinking that he hadn't seen her in Prineville, either. "I just got into town. I'm from Egan Valley."

"Why," she said, pleased, "that's where we're going to live. I'm Lynn Quaid. My father's up there now. Maybe you met him. Dan Quaid."

"Dan Quaid." The words were jolted out of him. "Yes, I met him."

He strode past her, almost running now, and found his room on down the hall. He went in and shut the door behind him. Dan Quaid would tell her he was Tobe Henderson's son and that he had stood beside his brother and hadn't lifted a hand when Bronc was fixing to shoot him.

Then a thought hit him, as wild a thought as had ever entered his mind. Dan Quaid would have to hire men to build a ranch from nothing. Maybe, if he could convince Quaid that he was not spying for his father, he could get a job with him. If he did, he would see Lynn every day and maybe he could prove he wasn't as awkward as he had appeared in the hall. One thing was sure. He'd be lined up against his father and brothers and that, he told himself, was exactly the way he wanted it.

Chapter 15

WHEN DAN QUAID reached Matt Runyan's cabin, Matt insisted that he take the bed. It was the only one in the cabin. Matt said he and Dawson could sleep in the barn. There was plenty of hay in the mow and they would be comfortable. Quaid argued with him, saying he wasn't one to drive a man out of his own bed, but he soon found out that it was futile to argue with Matt Runyan.

He pulled off his boots and sprawled across the bed, tired and sleepy and a little sick from the aches and pains of a dozen bruises. He heard Matt build a fire, then the sound of their voices, a low murmur as if they were a long way off, and suddenly he heard nothing. Matt let him sleep until the meal was ready, then woke him and told him to wash.

Quaid got up from the bed and sat down immediately, the room turning in front of him. He shook his head and waited a minute, then rose and walked slowly across the cabin to the bench that held the wash basin. Cold water and a little time cleared his head, and when he sat down at the table with Matt and Dawson, he discovered he was ravenously hungry.

When they were done eating, Matt leaned back

in his chair while the other two men filled their pipes. He said, "It's time to talk, Mr. Quaid. What we say tonight may determine our future as well as the valley's. Do you want to go back to bed or do you feel like sitting up?"

"I feel fine." Quaid struck a match and lighted his pipe. "I guess I won't be in A Number One shape for a while, but there's too much to do to sit around waiting till I feel good."

"Indeed there is," Matt said. "Well now, first I want you to understand that the original company which came into possession of what is now called the Cascade and Eastern Oregon Land Company's wagon road grant obtained it by fraud. The company was organized by a group of Willamette Valley business men way back in the 1860's. Unfortunately they had the ear of the governor and, also unfortunately, the law provided that the grant should be turned over to them when the governor certified that the company had fulfilled its contract.

"The point is that the company never did fulfill its contract and I believe never intended to. It did spend some money, perhaps $10,000, in building a road of sorts over the Cascades to the Deschutes River. But it was a different story from the Deschutes to the state line. They simply drove the wagon through the sagebrush and called the tracks they made a road.

"Now the joker is this. The governor never

135

inspected the road himself, but he sent out representatives who did. There was no state money to pay these men; therefore the company gave them their expense money and whatever wages they received. It was natural that they would favor the company and inform the governor that the road was built. The governor, in turn, certified that the road was completed and the company then received over 800,000 acres of land, much of it the best land in this part of the state.

"I moved to Egan Valley shortly after this happened, but I knew nothing about it at the time. Neither did Gabe Henderson, who was in the valley when I came. I settled on a choice quarter section just below the store. We naturally assumed we would eventually obtain title to our land by virtue of squatter's rights, but, years later after the country was surveyed, we learned we were on company land which was not open to entry.

"We fought it in the courts, Mr. Quaid, along with other men who were in the same boat. We fought it in the state legislature and we fought it in Congress. We enlisted the help of the biggest newspapers in the state and we finally persuaded the Department of the Interior, or more specifically, the General Land Office, to send a special agent out here to check on the grant personally.

"The agent they sent was a good man. I talked to him personally when he came through the valley, and I even rode with him for about fifty miles trying to find some evidence that a road had been built. There was no such evidence, Mr. Quaid, except for the few stakes which we were able to find and a small number of blazes on trees east of here where they climbed out of the valley.

"The report that he made was devastating. The government tied the land up in courts, but in the end the courts held that the land belonged to the company regardless of whether it fulfilled its part of the contract. It seems that when the governor certified that the road had been built, the law was satisfied and we were unable to put the land back in the public domain.

"When we knew we were whipped, I moved up here and I told Gabe he was foolish to stay on land he could not get a patent on. But he had put up most of the buildings you saw on the T Bar and he said he'd stay there till they moved him out. For years the original company did not try to sell the land. It actually refused to sell to small settlers like Gabe Henderson and me when we made a *bona fide* offer. They obviously had the idea that if they held on long enough, events would increase the value of their property and they could sell it as a bloc at a great profit. For this reason Henderson and none of the others were bothered by the law, although they were squatters and actually were trespassers." He nodded at Dawson. "All right, my friend, you can finish the story."

"It's short and sweet," Dawson said. "The company did not push sales for a time, although agents were stationed out here in various towns to look after the company's interest. Much of the land was leased to cowmen. We've had agents in Prineville for several years, and because they were not very astute, we might say, all they accomplished was to turn most of the people in the county against them. They did sell the section you want to a number of men who failed to stick, largely because of Mr. Runyan's efforts. No doubt Henderson helped."

"I might say at this point," Matt interrupted, "that Gabe saw things the way I did. We never used violence against anyone who came here as long as he was alive. All the settlers in the valley ran cattle on company land, so everyone had a selfish motive in keeping people out. My property was not involved, you understand, but after Gabe died, most of the people looked to me for leadership. We always won because we held together and ostracized the newcomers. We didn't let them come to our dances or church or school. We refused to exchange work with them. Orrie Bean even refused to sell anything to them.

"After Gabe died, Tobe was too impatient to follow such tactics. He and his boys beat up several men like they did you. We held with the Hendersons so the sheriff was never able to convict them, but last spring they would have lynched Sam Wardell if I hadn't arrived in time to save his life. We will not hold with Henderson any longer, Mr. Quaid. Even the valley is not worth a murder. Once a life is taken, there will be an avalanche of wholesale killings."

Dawson nodded. "That's where the shoe is pinching right now. When the Hill and Harriman companies began building their railroad up the Deschutes, we knew it was time to start a publicity campaign so the land could be sold.

"The men who own the company realize that using the law and asking the sheriff to evict the squatters will lead to bloodshed which will be in the headlines all over the country. Within a year we hope to bring 50,000 people to Central Oregon and we expect to sell most of them land. Obviously we won't even get the people out here if there is a lot of publicity given to bloodshed resulting from official action that we instituted. That's the reason Wardell picked you, Quaid. He's gambling that you will kill Tobe Henderson which will end the real resistance in the valley. Or, if Henderson kills you, Wardell can probably force the sheriff to arrest him. Maybe he won't be convicted, but he'll be out of circulation for a long time."

"He would be convicted," Matt said gravely.

"This is the part we really want you to know, Mr. Quaid. We are not going to oppose you. I intend to call a meeting of the valley people and I'm sure I can persuade all of them except Henderson to follow my orders. In fact, I have talked to them already along this line. We will never perjure ourselves again to keep Tobe or his sons out of jail. We've done everything we could and we've lost. We hate to admit it, but times are changing. Mr. Dawson assures me the company will deal fairly with everyone in the valley by selling to them at a nominal sum or paying for their improvements on an honest price level."

"This has been one of the big problems," Dawson said. "Wardell has not been willing to change policies. I understand he offered a fraction of what the improvements were worth, or offered to sell at a price that was too high for land the settlers had developed and were living on."

Quaid looked at one man and then the other, not sure that anything had been said that actually changed the situation. He would still buy the land and he would start to work at once in building a ranch, and he would still have to fight Tobe Henderson.

Finally Quaid said, "I'll go to Prineville tomorrow and see Wardell the first thing. I suppose he'd raise the price on me if he didn't think he had use for me."

Dawson's whiskery face broke into a grin. "That's exactly right. Close your deal immediately. Don't tell Wardell what's happening up here. What I'm most afraid of is that when Wardell sees this isn't working the way he planned, he'll send Pete Sloane up here to murder Henderson and work it so you'll be blamed. I suggest that you have someone with you all the time."

"Just one more thing before we go to bed," Matt said. "Rusty Henderson hates his father and his brothers, but mostly his father. This would not be hard for you to understand, Mr. Quaid, if you knew how he has been treated. He's in Prineville. He said he wasn't going to run and let people think he was a coward. The idea struck me that you would do well to hire him. He's a good boy and a hard worker."

Quaid shook his head. "That's a hell of an idea. I don't want any Henderson working for me."

"Rusty is not just any Henderson," Runyan said calmly. "He's much like his grandfather. Old Gabe was my friend. That's one reason I'd like to do something for Rusty. Maybe this is the way. He needs a home. Friends. People who can reach out and share what they have with him. I hope you're that big a man, Mr. Quaid."

"We'll see," Quaid said.

After the other two men had left the cabin and the lamp was dark, Quaid found himself lying awake thinking about it. He needed someone who knew the country and the people, and he had never fully trusted Pete Sloane. Now that he had been told Sloane was a company man, he had less reason to trust him. He had hired him last night. He would fire him tomorrow.

Rusty Henderson was a different proposition. Quaid would take him on Matt Runyan's say-so, but maybe young Henderson would not want to come back to Egan Valley and be forced into a position where he would have to fight his father and brothers.

Still, there was a kind of irony about it that tickled Quaid and made him think more of Runyan than ever. The old man was shrewd. There was more steel in him than Quaid had thought. Before he dropped off to sleep he made a decision. He would talk to the boy about it. Maybe hiring him would be one means of buying insurance. It seemed unlikely that Tobe Henderson would attack the Quaids if his own son was working for them.

Chapter 16

QUAID was back in Prineville by late afternoon the following day. He turned his bay over to the hostler in Barlow's livery stable and strode along the runway to the corral in the rear of the stable. He was tired and sore from both the riding and the beating the Hendersons had given him. What was worse, he had thought about his situation all day and even with help from Hank Dawson and Matt Runyan, he saw little chance of beating Tobe Henderson and his boys. Still, he could not turn back. He had wanted a challenge. Now he had it.

He found Johnny listening to a group of men talk about some horses Barlow was planning to buy from a rancher who lived up the Ochoco. He thought with a wry smile that Johnny was horse crazy. That was the reason he spent so much time here at Barlow's, which seemed to be the horse-trading center of Prineville. Well, Johnny would soon get his fill of horses if Quaid made the deal with Sam Wardell.

Johnny spun around when Quaid laid a hand on his shoulder. He started to say howdy, then he saw the bruises on his father's face and blurted, "What the hell happened to you, Dad? Meet up with a mountain lion?"

"You might say that," Quaid agreed. "Is Lynn at the hotel?"

"I guess so," Johnny said. "I ain't seen her since dinner. She was there then."

"Come on," Quaid said. "I want to have a family talk before we eat supper."

"Wait a minute, Dad." Johnny motioned toward another youth who was as tall and almost as slender as he was. "This is Rusty Henderson. Rusty, meet my dad."

Young Henderson hesitantly held his hand out. He said, "I wouldn't blame you if you didn't shake hands with me, Mr. Quaid. Not after what happened in the store."

Quaid smiled as he gripped Rusty's hand. He said, "I wouldn't have if I hadn't talked to Matt Runyan. From what he says I guess you've got more trouble than I have."

"I've got lots of trouble," Rusty said. "If I go back to Egan Valley I'll have a lot more, but that's what I want to do, Mr. Quaid. I'd like to work for you."

Funny how heredity worked, Quaid thought. Rusty showed no resemblance to Tobe Henderson or the two older boys, and there was none of the irritating truculence which was so evident in his father and brothers. He might have been just another young cowhand like most of the others scattered around the corral.

"Rusty knows horses," Johnny said eagerly.

"He sure made a ride this morning, the best I ever seen. They had a big black bruiser in the corral that Barlow had just bought and nobody could stay on him but Rusty. Golly, that was a ride."

"I haven't made the deal yet," Quaid said. "You're staying in town?"

"At the hotel," Rusty said. "I need a job, Mr. Quaid. Nobody will give me anything. They're afraid of Pa."

"They've got a right to be," Quaid said. "I'll let you know." He jerked his head at Johnny. "Come on." They walked through the archway to the street and when they turned toward the hotel, Quaid asked, "You appear to like young Henderson."

"I sure do," Johnny answered. "Lynn does, too. She ran into him in the hall. I bet she done it on purpose. Mom says she's too forward."

Quaid sighed. "Sometimes I'm inclined to agree," he said.

Quaid found Angie and Lynn in his and Angie's room. Lynn was sprawled across the bed; Angie was sitting beside the window, some sewing on her lap. She ran to him and kissed him, and then he held her in his arms for a long minute. When he let her go, she was crying.

"Now Angie," he said, "I didn't figure coming back would make you cry."

"I'm sorry." She wiped her eyes on her handkerchief and tried to smile. "I've been worried.

That cowboy Sloane said that you were all right, but he acted funny, as if you'd had some trouble. He wouldn't tell me anything. He just . . ." Then she saw the marks on his face and she stopped. "What happened, Dan?"

"I'm going to tell you," he said. "That's why I fetched Johnny. We've got some talking to do."

He glanced at Lynn who was sitting up, smiling at him. "Dad, you look like you've been in a fight. Aren't you too old for that?"

He frowned, not sure whether she was being facetious or not. He said, "Right now I feel like I'm a hundred years old." He closed the door and walked to the window, then turned so he faced them. "You're right, Lynn. I have been in a fight, and if we move to Egan Creek, I'll be in a lot more. So will Johnny if he goes with me."

He turned his gaze to his son. "This isn't a school kid fracas, and it's not the kind of row we used to have in the Willamette Valley if our bull got in with the neighbor's cows or something like that. We can get killed, Johnny. Both of us." He paused, and added, "In fact, the odds are that we will. That's why I'm not telling you to go with me. I'd like to have you, but you'll have to make the decision."

Johnny's gaze locked with his. He said, "Of course I'm going with you."

"Good," Quaid said, sensing that the boy was hurt because his courage had been doubted. "I

146

was sure you would." He turned to Angie who was staring at the sewing on her lap. "You and Lynn will have to stay here in town for a while till Johnny and me get the cabin fixed up and a couple more rooms built onto it. Maybe we can rent a house for you. It would be nicer than this hotel room."

She looked up then and he saw that tears were in her eyes again. "I thought you would say something like that. Well, we're not staying here. We're going with you and there's nothing you can do to stop us. If you think I'm going to sit in a hotel room or a rented house and worry about you and Johnny every hour of the day and most of the night . . ."

She couldn't go on. Lynn said, "That's right, Dad. We've talked about it. We're part of the family just as much as Johnny."

He gave them his back for a moment, emotion ruling him so completely that for a time he couldn't speak. These were the people he loved most in all the world. He was responsible for them being here, for uprooting them from a safe and sane life in the Willamette Valley. If anything happened to them . . . He turned, unwilling to face that possibility.

"I'd better tell you what I ran into," he said.

He did, sparing them nothing, and when he was done, Johnny said, "So that's what he meant when he said something about what happened in the store. He'd have let his brother murder you."

"I blamed him then," Quaid said, "but I don't now. He hadn't made the break with his family yet. That's a hard thing to do, even hating his father and brothers the way he does."

"You haven't told us the important thing, Dan," Angie said. "You've told us how you were almost killed and beaten half to death and how you shot at other men for the first time in your life. . . ."

"Not to kill them," he broke in.

"But you could have killed them," she insisted, "and you know you will if you buy that place. You knew you might run into something like this when you left the Willamette Valley. You . . ."

"Not this bad," he broke in again. "I never dreamed I'd find a situation like this in a country that has law and order."

"I know you better than that, Dan," she said, smiling. "Maybe you didn't really dream it, but you were hoping this is what you would find. You're a pioneer at heart and you should have been born fifty years before you were. Life was too mild for you in the Willamette Valley. Now you've found what you were looking for. . . ."

"Angie, it isn't so," he interrupted. "I don't know what's got into you. I didn't . . ."

"Let me finish," she said. "There's just one thing to consider and you haven't talked about it yet. If there is danger, we'll meet it. If the people in Egan Valley won't have anything to do with us, we'll live by ourselves. I say there's just one thing. Is that piece of land exactly what you want?"

"Yes," he said without hesitation. "It was so exactly what I wanted that I had a crazy notion I'd been there before. Or that I'd seen it before and I know I hadn't. I guess I'd just dreamed about it."

"All right, Dan," she said. "Go see Wardell and buy it, but don't talk any more about leaving Lynn and me in town. Of course I'll be afraid, and there'll be times when I'll wish I was back home and maybe I'll say things to you I shouldn't, but I won't mean them. If I gave way to every fear I have, I'd never have married you in the first place. And there's another thing. The children take after you. They aren't scaredy cats like me."

"We're pioneers, too," Lynn said, and laughed.

"Not me," Johnny said. "I just want to be a cowboy."

Angie was right. The children weren't afraid. She was right about herself, too. If she had permitted her fears to rule her, she wouldn't have married him.

"I'll go see Wardell now," he said, "and then we'll have supper."

That night he held Angie in his arms and loved her, and he thought that in all the world he was the luckiest of men. Courage, he knew, was not a matter of being unafraid. Rather, it was the refusal to let fears rule a person's action. By that standard, he told himself, Angie was a very brave woman.

Chapter 17

PETE SLOANE was in the Stockmen's Bar when he saw Dan Quaid ride into town. He was surprised. If the plan had worked and Quaid had shot and killed Tobe Henderson, Quaid probably would not be riding into town. In fact, Sloane was surprised to see Quaid at all, for he had figured the odds favored Henderson and his boys outlasting Quaid. If that had happened, the company would have had the weapon it needed to get rid of the Hendersons.

Sloane was certain that the murder of a man like Dan Quaid would have resulted in a conviction. Wardell had played it smart, sending Quaid to talk to Rufe Langer and Billy Mason and to have the run-in with Tobe Henderson and his boy, Shep, here in the Stockmen's Bar. Well, the Hendersons hadn't murdered Quaid. That was sure, but there was still a chance it had gone the other way.

Sloane took a bottle and glass to a table near the window and sat down to watch the street. He was not surprised when he saw Quaid go into the company's office, but he was at the length of time he was there, and he was even more surprised when Quaid left the office and came directly to the saloon. Quaid stepped inside, saw Sloane, and sat down at his table.

"How much do I owe you?" Quaid asked.

"I just started working for you," Sloane said. "I didn't figure it was pay day yet."

"You started and you stopped," Quaid said. "I'm paying you off and I figure it's good riddance. You'd have been a hell of a lot more honest if you'd said to start with that you were a company man instead of giving me that song and dance about being out of a job."

"Where'd you hear I was a company man?" Sloane demanded.

"Dawson told me," Quaid answered. "Likewise he told me'n Matt Runyan that he worked for the company, too. Now tell me how much I owe you and I'll pay you off and then you keep out of my way. I've bought the section of land I was after, and from now on I don't want to have anything to do with you or Wardell or the company."

"Now hold on," Sloane said. "You're going to need us when it comes to bucking Tobe Henderson. The beating they gave you was just a taste of what you'll get if you move up there. All I was trying to do was to help you. . . ."

"Help me, hell," Quaid said angrily. "From what Dawson says, I'll live longer if I never get any more of your help."

"Just what did Dawson say?"

"He told me a lot of things, things I should have guessed because Wardell said the same, but he put a little different focus on it. Dawson said that Wardell would probably send you back to the valley to murder Tobe Henderson and work it so I'd be held for the killing. He said Wardell was using me to pull the company's chestnuts out of the fire. He was going to wire the company about the way things were going. I hope he does, Sloane, and that you and Wardell both get fired."

Sloane was jolted by this, but he didn't let Quaid see it in his face. He shrugged and said pleasantly, "Maybe Dawson will get fired instead. He's been asking for it." He rolled a cigarette, and asked, "Want a drink? I'll get another glass if . . ."

"No. I'm just trying to pay you off and get rid of you."

Sloane leaned forward. "Look, Quaid. Dawson's a sore head. He hates me and he's jealous of Wardell. Sure, maybe I should have told you I was a company man, but in the past it's always worked out better if nobody knew. Now don't forget I saved your life. . . ."

"Did you now?" Quaid rose. "How do I know you did?"

"You calling me a liar?"

"That's exactly what I'm calling you," Quaid said. "Everything you've said to me since you took Lynn riding has been a lie. Why wouldn't this yarn about saving my life be the same?"

Wardell would have his hide, Sloane thought. He'd been a fool. He should have denied everything Dawson had told Quaid. Wardell had planned this so carefully and now it probably wouldn't work out. If Dawson did wire the company . . . !

Suddenly frustration and the whisky he'd been drinking was too much for Sloane. He jumped up and shouted, "You son of a bitch. I ain't standing still for that talk."

His gun was half out of leather when Quaid, moving like a cat, threw out his left hand and grabbed the gun barrel in the same instant that he caught the brim of Sloan's hat with his right and jerked it down over the company man's eyes. He wrenched the gun from Sloane's hand and threw it across the room.

"I guess I don't owe you anything," Quaid said. "The company can pay you wages. Just stay away from me and don't come around my daughter, either."

Sloane heard a man at the bar snicker. He yanked off his hat and threw the table sideways and lunged at Quaid, his right fist coming up in a punch that would have knocked Quaid cold if it had landed. Quaid ducked the uppercut. The wild swinging blow pulled Sloane off balance and left him wide open. Quaid drove a sledging fist to his stomach and another to his jaw, and Sloane hit the floor. He wasn't knocked out, but he couldn't move, either. He lay there, fighting for breath. He saw Quaid's feet not more than two feet from him; he raised his head enough to follow Quaid's legs as far as his waist, then his head dropped back to the floor.

The barman said, "You pack a wallop for a Willamette Valley greenhorn."

"I'm getting over the greenhorn stage pretty fast," Quaid said. "I hope this bastard remembers my wallop and tells Sam Wardell about it."

He wheeled and strode out. Sloane struggled to his feet and leaned against the wall. The room was a giant top that was whirling in front of him and threatening to throw him far out into space. One of the men at the bar, a fellow named Wash Morgan who worked in Barlow's stable, asked, "How are you hooked up with Wardell?"

"I ain't," Sloane said. "Quaid must have been drunk."

Morgan laughed derisively. "You're crazy. A drunk couldn't handle himself the way Quaid done."

Sloane let it go. He'd had enough fighting for one evening. He crossed the room, which had finally stopped turning, and picked up his revolver. He went outside, walking slowly for he was still having trouble with his breathing.

He considered hunting Quaid up and telling him to get a gun. Then his head began to clear and the anger that had been a red, compelling fury lost its fine edge. Quaid could be taken care of any time. Dawson was the one. Henry Oglethorpe Dawson, the company's pet. Going to wire the company, was he? Wardell would like to know about that.

He walked around town until it was dark. He hadn't eaten supper, but he didn't think he could keep anything down. Quaid's fist had hit him like a mule kick. He got his horse from Barlow's stable and rode to the back of Wardell's place. He dismounted and whistled. He watched Mrs. Wardell move from the table in the kitchen to the stove and back. Then Sam Wardell appeared on the back porch, stood there a moment talking to his wife, and finally stepped to the ground and crossed the yard to the barn.

"What the hell, Pete?" Wardell demanded in a low tone. "I told you this was dangerous. I don't want you seen here. Even my wife shouldn't know. . . ."

"It ain't half as dangerous as what's going to happen if we don't do something and do it fast," Sloane broke in. "Dawson's fixing to wire the company about what's going on here and what do you think he'll say?"

"What's he got to wire the company about?" Wardell asked. "He'll just get himself fired if he tries to cut my throat."

"You think so, do you?" Sloane said. "Well, I had a talk with your man Quaid. He says he bought the land."

"He came in late this afternoon and closed the deal, but . . ."

"Dawson spilled the beans to him," Sloane interrupted. "All the beans. He told Quaid the company was using him to pull its chestnuts out of the fire and that you'd probably send me to the valley to kill Henderson and fix it so he'd be blamed."

Surprised, Wardell said, "The hell he did! What's got into Hank?"

"I'd say he was after your job," Sloane said. "I never have trusted him and you know it. And another thing. When I talked to him on Crooked River he said he had his belly full of your tactics and he was going to speak his piece to the Prineville newspaper. He said Quaid was a lamb going to slaughter. I said it sounded like he'd got religion and he said he finally had."

Wardell was silent for a time. Sloane could not see his face in the darkness, so he had no idea what was going through the man's mind. Finally he blurted, "Sam, maybe you think you can pull more wires than Dawson can, but your record ain't been real good here, neither. If it hadn't been for Matt Runyan, you'd be dead, and I've got a hunch Dawson will work on that angle. You came here to change the public's picture of the company, but you've got a rope burn on your neck to prove you ain't changed nothing. If Dawson blabs all he knows to that damned newspaper . . ."

"You're working too hard at this, Pete," Wardell said. "I've played this game a little too tight like my predecessors did and that's been a mistake, although I'm not sure that anything I could have said or done would have changed Tobe Henderson. I picked Quaid for a purpose and it may still work. However, I'm not going to stand still for Dawson, working both ends against the middle and cutting my throat."

"There's one way to stop him," Sloane said. "It would be a pleasure to do it. If he's still in the valley, I can find him."

"All right," Wardell said. "I refuse to be involved personally, but this is your game. If you want to play it, I can't stop you."

"But you won't order it?"

"Of course not. We're all company men and we're supposed to work as a team. If Dawson has got religion as he said and tries to tell the company how to operate, he'll wind up cutting his own throat."

"You're a fool, Sam," Sloane said bitterly. "A chicken-livered fool. Dawson told me you wouldn't do your own killing. He said you'd send me to do it, but you don't even have the guts to do that. Well, all I'm asking is that you see to it when the time comes that the big boys know Dawson was selling 'em out and I saved their hides by getting rid of the bastard. And another thing. After I get Dawson, I'm going after Quaid.

Henderson will swing for it, and I'll be out of the country a long time before that."

He mounted and rode down the alley. Wardell stood there, pulling steadily on his pipe, his mouth tight. The company was well aware that men like Pete Sloane could be bought any time and anywhere but men like Sam Wardell were hard to come by. So was a man like Henry Oglethorpe Dawson. But he was a dead man, a death that in no way could be pinned on Sam Wardell.

"Sam, you still out there?" his wife called from the back porch.

"I'm here," he answered. "Just getting some fresh air."

"You've had time to get a bushel of it," she said petulantly. "Come in and dry the dishes for me."

"All right, honey," he said.

He knocked his pipe out against his heel and slipped it into his pocket. He started back across the yard when suddenly his smoldering anger flared into a blaze. So Dawson thought he would never do his own killing. Well, if Dawson succeeded in getting the agent's job, which was certainly what he was after, he was in for a surprise. He'd find out if he ever walked into the Prineville office and said he was taking over.

Chapter 18

THE SUN was a red ball showing above the ridges of the Blue Mountains when Quaid rapped on Rusty Henderson's door. He called, "It's Dan Quaid. Come on down to the dining room and I'll buy you your breakfast. I want to talk to you."

"I'll be right down," Rusty said.

Quaid waited in the lobby. He still hadn't made up his mind about the boy. It simply wasn't logical to think that any good could be found in one of Tobe Henderson's sons, good as measured by Dan Quaid's standards at least. The thought entered his mind that this might be a trick, that perhaps Henderson had sent his boy to town to get a job with him and then betray him.

No, that didn't make sense because Tobe Henderson wasn't a sly and scheming man like Sam Wardell. Besides, Quaid sensed an honesty in the boy that he couldn't believe was play acting. More than that, Johnny and Lynn liked him, and Quaid told himself that they would have felt dishonesty in him if he was masquerading as something he wasn't. But more than anything else was Matt Runyan's opinion of him. He had told Quaid that he would do well to hire the boy, and Quaid was convinced that Matt Runyan was the one man in the valley he could trust.

Rusty came down the stairs then and Quaid led the way into the dining room. They sat down at the table and gave their orders. Then Quaid asked, "Why do you want to work for me, Rusty? Or maybe the question is why do you want to go back to Egan Valley?"

Rusty's gaze locked with Quaid's. He said gravely, "I guess you're not sure you can trust me."

"It's a reasonable doubt," Quaid said. "I know what your dad and brothers will do to me if they can."

"Yeah, it's a reasonable doubt all right," Rusty agreed, and stared at the table. "If you hire me, Mr. Quaid, it'll have to be on faith. I just don't figure I can make you understand how it is with me, except maybe to say I've got to have a job and Pa's got everybody hereabouts buffaloed."

"Try," Quaid urged.

Sweat made a bright shine on Rusty's face, although the morning was a cool one. He said finally, "I guess I was Ma's boy, not Pa's. I mean, I don't hold with the things Pa does any more'n Ma did when she was alive. Like beating you up and fixing to hang Sam Wardell. You see, I've talked to Matt Runyan a lot of times and he's told me about Grandpa. I remember him pretty good, too. Matt says I'm kind o' like him. He never done the things Pa does. He had ways of getting folks out of the valley without hanging 'em or beating 'em to death like Pa done to you."

"It's still not good enough."

"I know," Rusty said. "There's more, a hell of a lot more, but it's hard to tell it. You see, I've hated Pa since I was little. I hated Shep and Bronc, too. I was never big enough to handle 'em and they was scared of each other, I guess, so they always took their cussedness out on me. Before Ma died, she told me I could find beauty and love if I looked for it, but I'd never find it on the T Bar. She was telling me to leave home, I guess, but I never got enough gumption to do it till now."

He started making a criss-cross pattern on the table cloth with a finger nail, his eyes on the window to his right. "Pa killed my mother. Oh, he didn't shoot her or beat her to death, but he worked her too hard and nothing that she done satisfied him. After a while it seemed like she didn't see no sense in living, so she just died."

He paused, his finger nail still moving back and forth across the tablecloth. "I'd have left home sooner, but I wasn't sure I could make a living or even get a job. Well, I got so I figured it was better to starve to death somewhere else than to go on living on the T Bar. When I was little I used to see pictures in the sky, among the clouds, you know, and I'd try to tell about 'em and Pa would whip me for seeing things that wasn't there." He brought his gaze back to Quaid's face. "I've got reason to hate him, believe me."

Quaid nodded, satisfied. "I reckon you have, Rusty. All right, I'll give you a job."

"Thanks, Mr. Quaid. I'll work hard." Their orders came, but Rusty didn't touch his food for a time. He said, "What finally triggered it off and fixed it so I got up and left was standing beside Bronc in Orrie Bean's store when he was going to kill you, and me not having guts enough to stop him when I knowed I should. When I got home with Bronc and he told Pa what had happened, Pa allowed I was a stinking coward and wasn't worth being called a Henderson. He figured I should of done something to Dawson so Bronc would have had a chance to pull his gun. Well, I guess that's the real reason I've got to go back to the valley. I aim to show Pa I ain't no coward, and I aim to show him I'm going to live my way, not his and Bronc's and Shep's."

"That's every man's right," Quaid said. He was ashamed then, for he had drawn this out of the boy when it was not really his business, and he felt as if he had forced Rusty to undress and now the boy stood naked before him. He added quickly, "I didn't figure you for a coward. It takes guts to run away from home and more guts to go back afterwards."

"You'd best know one thing," Rusty said as if he hadn't heard. "Pa will never sell his improvements to the company and he won't go broke paying the big price the company asks for the land. He'll go on fighting as long as he's alive and he'll figure you're his enemy same as the company is. Having me work for you ain't gonna keep him from giving you hell, so don't figure on it."

"I didn't," Quaid said, and then remembered it was a lie, for he had thought of Rusty as being insurance against Henderson's attack. Now, after what the boy had told him, he knew that it was a futile hope just as Rusty had said. He finished his ham and eggs, and stirred his second cup of coffee as he said, "I've got to buy some horses. Seems like I heard about a rancher up the Ochoco who had some."

Rusty nodded. "Yeah, Wash Morgan was telling me about 'em. He works for Barlow, you know. This fellow's name is Josh Kinnear. He raises horses to sell, but he don't break 'em to ride. He's got about twenty, most of 'em geldings. Wash says they're good stock and Barlow was going to buy 'em, but he never bothered to ride up there to see 'em, so you might just as well have 'em."

"I don't claim to be a bronc buster," Quaid said hesitantly. "Johnny's not, either."

"I can break 'em for you," Rusty said without the slightest hint of bragging. "I hit Barlow up for a job and he turned me down, saying Pa let him alone and he let Pa alone and that was the way

164

he wanted it. Well, I was down there yesterday with Johnny when Wash tried to ride that big black Barlow had just bought. He didn't last long. Barlow got on him and the next thing you know Barlow was lying on his back in the middle of the corral sunning himself. Then I tried and I rode him, Mr. Quaid. I don't figure Josh Kinnear has got anything half as ornery as that black."

"All right," Quaid said. "Your job will be to break that string of horses. Now there's another thing. Besides you and me and Johnny, I'll need one more man, a good man who won't quit me or sell out to your pa if it comes down to that. You know of anybody?"

Rusty nodded. "This Wash Morgan I was talking about, Barlow don't pay him much and I know he's looking around. He's mad at Pa and Bronc and Shep, too. They gave him a beating in the Stockmen's Bar a few months ago and he'd like another run at it."

"I'll talk to him," Quaid said. "You go up and roust Johnny out of bed while I see your friend Morgan."

He paid for the meal, and left the dining room, and walked rapidly to Barlow's livery stable. A tall man, about twenty-five years old, was cleaning out stalls. Quaid asked, "You Wash Morgan?"

The tall man nodded. "That's me."

Quaid held out his hand. "I'm Dan Quaid. I've

bought a place in Egan Valley and I need a good man. Rusty Henderson said you were one."

Morgan shook hands, leaned the shovel against the side of the stall, walked to the front of the stable, took his hat off a nail on the wall and put it on. He said, "You just hired yourself a man, Mr. Quaid. I was in the Stockmen's Bar yesterday when you handled Pete Sloane. I'd admire to work for you."

"Now wait a minute," Quaid said. "You can't just walk off and leave Barlow without giving him a warning."

"He's been warned for a week or more," Morgan said. "He owes me for two months' wages and the only way I'm going to collect it is to take one of his horses and saddles. I was quitting tonight anyhow. You ain't asked for advice yet, but I'll give you some anyhow. Don't buy anything from Abe Barlow, not unless you're prepared to haggle with him for two, three days. Otherwise he'll trade you right out of the shirt you're wearing."

"Rusty was telling me about a man named Kinnear who has a horse ranch up the Ochoco."

Morgan nodded. "He's got good stock and he'll be damned glad to sell them for what Barlow offered him if you'll come and get 'em. I'll ride up there with you today if you want me to. That is, as soon as I settle up with Abe which ain't gonna be easy."

166

"I figured to buy a couple of wagons and two teams," Quaid said. "We'll have to lay in some supplies and I'll need tools and such."

"I can help you," Morgan said. "They'll over-charge you if you let 'em 'cause the story's around about you and nobody allows you'll last the year out, so if they can soak you now, they ain't worrying about no repeat business."

"What about you?" Quaid asked. "You know what you're getting into if you sign on with me?"

"I know," Morgan said. "That's why I'm signing on. You're a fighting man, Mr. Quaid. Egan Valley ain't seen nobody like you lately. Last night I bet $100 that you wouldn't hang and rattle." A grin tightened his lips as he added, "I'd kind o' like to help myself win that bet."

Quaid thought about what Morgan had said as they rode up the Ochoco later that morning. "You're a fighting man, Mr. Quaid." They were words he liked to hear. He wondered what had happened to him since he had left the Willamette Valley. Nobody had ever said that to him before. But then no one had ever had reason to before.

Chapter 19

HANK DAWSON stayed at Matt Runyan's place while Runyan visited all the valley settlers and told them there would be a meeting in the schoolhouse at ten on Saturday morning. Some said they'd be there, others simply nodded, giving no hint of their feelings or whether they had any idea what the meeting was about, but none were openly hostile except Tobe Henderson.

"It's come to the parting of the ways," Runyan told Dawson Friday night when he returned to his cabin. "Tobe will be there, but we'd be better off if he didn't come. Well, this should have been settled a long time ago. If I wasn't a weak man, I'd have forced it before this, but I guess I'm like most people. I'd rather get along with my neighbors than shove an issue at them."

Dawson looked at him curiously. "Matt, if you're a weak man, I hate to consider what the rest of us are."

The truth is we're all weak," Runyan said gravely, "but we think it's a disgrace to admit it, whereas the truth is and that weakness is sometimes more of a virtue than strength. In Henderson's case what he considers strength is damn fool stubbornness and it's actually a weakness. He's afraid to back up or change course because someone might call him a coward or an appeaser, so he'll go right down the line if it kills him."

"Which it may do," Dawson said. "What do you expect in the morning?"

"Hard to tell," Runyan answered, "but we'll know the instant you tell the crowd you're a company man."

"Maybe you'd better tell them," Dawson said. "If they won't listen to you, they sure won't listen to me."

"All right," Runyan said. "I'll tell them when I introduce you."

Dawson slept very little that night. He honestly didn't think that the valley people would listen to Matt Runyan after they heard that a man they had known as an itinerant peddler was actually a company representative. All that it would take to turn the crowd into a lynch mob would be for Tobe Henderson to open his mouth a few times.

Dawson's mind had not changed when he sat beside Runyan in the front of the schoolhouse the following morning and looked at the people before him. He didn't carry a gun on his hip because Runyan had told him that no one would be armed except Henderson and his boys, and if the people saw a gun on Dawson, they would decide he was not here out of friendship and good will.

On the other hand, he had no intention of letting

the Hendersons hang him as they had attempted to lynch Sam Wardell. He had therefore slipped his revolver inside his shirt, telling himself he would shoot Tobe Henderson before he'd let the man put a rope on his neck.

By ten o'clock the room was packed with thirty or more men and boys. As was customary with settler meetings in the valley, no women were there. Henderson and his sons stood with their backs to the rear wall, all three grinning derisively as they looked, over the heads of the seated men, at Runyan who rose and moved to stand behind the teacher's desk. Orrie Bean sat in the front row, his face so impassive that Dawson could not tell what was in his mind.

Runyan rapped on the desk top for silence, then said, "I have not told any of you what the purpose of this meeting was, but I'm sure you have all guessed that it had to do with the company and its claim to some of your land. This is a situation that we can't allow to go on indefinitely. . . ."

"Why the hell can't we?" Henderson bellowed. "Do you think you're God that you can tell us what to do about our homes when a thieving son-of-a-bitching outfit like the company is trying to run us off our land?"

Runyan leaned on the desk, his hands gripping the edge so tightly that his knuckles were white. He said, "Tobe, you will address the chair properly or leave the meeting."

Henderson laughed contemptuously and stepped forward, his big hands shoved inside his waistband. "You and who else is going to make me, old man?"

Orrie Bean rose and turned to face Henderson. "We will, Tobe. All of us."

Other men nodded and several said, "You're damned right, Orrie."

Henderson looked as if he'd been slapped in the face. He opened his mouth to say something, then closed it without saying a word. His muddy brown eyes narrowed, his great jaw jutted forward another quarter of an inch. Then he moved back to the wall and stood motionless. Orrie Bean sat down, and for the first time Dawson began to breathe naturally. Most of these people had lived in a state of war for years. Perhaps they were tired of it and this was the proper moment to make an offer, a moment in which they might listen.

"I was saying that we cannot allow this situation to go on indefinitely," Runyan said. "Our world is changing whether we want it to or not. Just one thing is responsible for it; that's the railroad which is being pushed up the Deschutes and which eventually will come into Prineville and possibly on up the Crooked River. People are bound to pour into Central Oregon by the thousands. The company wants to take advantage of this situation to sell its land, but it won't be easy if there is a period of lawlessness that is reported in newspapers all over the United States. That's why I'm convinced that if we are ever to get a decent offer from the company, it's right now."

He motioned for Dawson to stand beside him. "You have all met Hank Dawson, but he's not the peddler we thought he was. Actually he is a field representative of the C. and E. O. Land Company. . . ."

"By God, a spy," Henderson roared as he lunged up the aisle. "Get your rope, Shep. We'll hang this bastard before he says a word."

"Address the chair," Runyan shouted, pounding the table. "Go back to where you were, Tobe."

But Henderson didn't stop. Bronc was a step behind him. Dawson saw Shep dart outside. He'd be back in a matter of seconds with a rope. Not even Orrie Bean moved. The seated men remained motionless, mouths open, eyes wide with shock.

Runyan stepped in front of Henderson, shouting again, "Go on back, Tobe."

Henderson struck him on the side of the face, knocking him aside. Dawson had his hand inside his shirt, gripping the butt of his gun. Now he pulled it out and lined it on Henderson's belly. He said, "I didn't come here for trouble, but I don't propose for you to put a rope on my neck. You'll get a slug in your guts if you keep coming, Henderson."

Henderson stopped within five feet of Dawson, his eyes on the cocked revolver. He put out a hand and stopped Bronc who was pushing up behind him. For a moment there was complete silence in the room, then Dawson said, "You might have a chance if I shot you in the head or even the chest, but I'll put this slug right in your guts if you keep crowding me."

Runyan grabbed Henderson's arm. "Go on back, Tobe."

Henderson jerked free and wheeled so that his back was to Dawson. He shouted, "He's a company man. You boys heard Matt say it as plain as I did. He knew it all the time. He must be in it, too. Hang 'em, I say. Hang both of 'em."

"Funny that you think Matt's playing the company's game," Dawson said. "By the same token you deserve hanging, too. You gave Pete Sloane work and he's a company man."

Shep, who had come in with a coiled rope in his hands, stopped just inside the doorway. Slowly Henderson turned to Dawson. He said, "You're lying. You're lying to save your own neck."

"If I was that anxious to save my neck," Dawson said, "I wouldn't be here making you men an offer. I'd let you lose everything you've got, which is exactly what you deserve, and it's probably what will happen. But your neighbors have a right to get a better deal. Sloane's a company man, all right. He followed Dan Quaid up here. After you beat Quaid up, Sloane got him out of the valley and hid him in a cave. That's how Quaid was able to get back to the rim the next day and shoot your place up."

Orrie Beam rose and motioned to the men beside him. He said, "Tobe don't want nothing but to raise hell all the time, so he'd better get out of the meeting. He can do as he damn pleases. As for me, I don't like the company and I don't like Sam Wardell and I hate this red-headed peddler who claims he's a company man, but if he's here to make an offer, I'd be a fool not to listen."

Other men rose and stood beside him, stirred into action by what he had said. Dawson again thought that this was the right time to make an offer, that every man here except Tobe Henderson was tired of the strain and anxiety that had been faced for so many years.

"You're fools," Henderson bellowed. "If it hadn't been for me, this valley would have been overrun years ago and we'd have lost our homes before some of you were even born. Why, if it hadn't been for me and my pa . . ."

"Your pa, yes," Orrie Bean interrupted. "You, no. Matt Runyan's the one who kept this valley from being overrun. If he'd let you string Sam Wardell up like you tried to do and wanted to do with Dawson just now, we'd be out of this valley and some of us in jail. Now get out of here, Tobe, and let the banty rooster have his say."

Henderson swung around to face Dawson. "To hell with your say. You won't make no deal with me, and I don't figure on letting your man Quaid live here, neither. Tell him when you see him."

"You can tell him yourself," Dawson said. "He's on his way up here now."

"Then we'll turn him around," Henderson said.

He stalked past Bronc and Shep, the boys following. Presently the men inside the schoolhouse heard the drum of hoofs that gradually faded as the Hendersons rode away. Dawson cocked his head, listening. They were riding south toward the Narrows, not the T Bar, and he wondered about it.

"Go ahead," Bean said. "You can speak your piece now."

Dawson took a long breath. He wiped the sweat from his face with his sleeve. This had been close, even closer than he had expected. He could have shot and killed Tobe Henderson, but he could not have saved himself. By making Henderson a martyr, he would have turned every man in the room against him, perhaps even Matt Runyan, and they would have finished the job Henderson had tried to start.

He moistened his dry lips. He said, "I'm a lawyer. I do some legal work for the company in the San Francisco office, but I'm also a field man. I was sent here to make a study of your improvements so I could give a first hand report to the company, but I've decided not to give my report. Not now, anyhow. I'm not in sympathy with Sam Wardell and Pete Sloane and their way of operating because I don't think it's to the best interest of the company.

"I can't make any promises, but I am going to wire the main office in San Francisco and I will write at length urging that I be empowered to make those of you who are living on company land an honest offer. Or, and I believe most of you prefer this, to put a fair price on your land so you can buy it from the company. By fair I mean what unimproved land is worth, not what it is worth after you've worked your tail off for years making it your homes."

He was surprised when they cheered him. Bean said, "Dawson, that's the first sensible thing I ever heard a company man say."

"I believe I can convince the company that this is the proper course," Dawson said. "The men who direct the company's policy realize that this is a strategic moment. In return I expect you folks to stop feuding with people like Dan Quaid who buy from the company."

"That's fair enough," a man named Pat O'Brien said. "I reckon we all know we can't go on living in the past like Tobe Henderson wants us to. It's worth forgetting my pride to get a deed for my land. But there's one thing you ain't said. In your opinion what is a fair price? I mean, in dollars?"

"Again I can't make any promises," Dawson said. "Remember I'm bucking Sam Wardell. He's like the other agents who have been here. They want to turn in all the profit they can for the company. On paper that makes their records look good in the San Francisco office. All I can say is that my recommendation will be to let you buy for $2.00 an acre."

The sigh that rose from the crowd was a long, sustained sound. Then O'Brien said, "A heap of trouble would have been avoided if they'd sent you here in the first place, Mr. Dawson. It wasn't just principle we was fighting for, though I reckon that was part of it. Mostly the trouble has been over the offers they've made. They wanted to stick us for the work we'd done on our own places. They wanted to stick us bad."

"I didn't realize . . ."

The sound of a shot came to Dawson from somewhere down the valley, then another. He glanced at Runyan, wondering uneasily if the Hendersons had started out to turn Dan Quaid back and had murdered him instead.

He heard no more shooting, so he went on, "I didn't realize until I came here as a peddler that this valley had been improved as much as it had. The agents kept sending in reports that you were squatters and should be treated accordingly. You were to be driven off the company land if it could be done without creating too much bad publicity for the company. No agent ever figured out how to do it. That's why you've been allowed to stay here and it's why I was sent. It is only recently that someone in San Francisco figured out that the reason your ranches are valuable is that you've made them that way. This is a point Sam Wardell has not been willing to concede."

Runyan stepped up beside Dawson. "The purpose of the meeting has been accomplished, so a motion for adjournment is in order."

Dawson was detained for a long time by O'Brien and several other settlers who wanted to talk. They assured him that no one except Tobe Henderson would hold out against buying if the company agreed to the $2.00 per acre price. Orrie Bean had left without saying a word to Dawson. Dawson told himself he was a pessimist, but he could not quite shake off the fear that Tobe Henderson would soon beat the other settlers back into line. He wasn't sure, either, that Orrie Bean or any of the settlers except Runyan would welcome Dan Quaid and his family to the valley.

When he was finally able to leave the schoolhouse with Matt Runyan, he saw the Hendersons riding toward the settlement from the direction of the Narrows. Tobe was leading a horse with a man tied face down across the saddle. Dawson reached inside his shirt and drew his revolver, telling himself in a quick flare of passionate anger that he would shoot Tobe

Henderson out of his saddle if they had murdered Dan Quaid.

The settlers who had lingered to talk to Dawson crowded around him and Runyan as the Hendersons pulled up. Tobe dropped the reins of the horse that carried the dead man.

"We started for Prineville figuring to turn Quaid back," Tobe said in a flat, expressionless voice, "but we ran into this bastard riding up through the Narrows. He pulled his gun on us, so I plugged him." He nodded at Dawson. "We decided we'd let Quaid come on in, but I don't figure he'll stay."

The Hendersons turned their horses and rode toward the T Bar. Runyan strode to the dead man and lifted his head. Shocked, he wheeled to face the others. "It's Pete Sloane."

Dawson, remembering that he had told the Hendersons that Sloane was a company man, knew that indirectly he was responsible for Sloane's death. He said, "My guess is he never went for his gun. They murdered him."

Troubled, Runyan shook his head as he stared at the departing Hendersons. "We can't prove it. All we can do is to let Billy Mason know."

It was true, Dawson knew, and he wondered if anything would ever really change in Egan Valley as long as Tobe Henderson was alive.

Chapter 20

QUAID camped Saturday night on Crooked River some distance below its junction with Egan Creek. With Wash Morgan's help, he had shopped around until he had bought two wagons and teams at a reasonable price. Both wagons were heavily loaded with food, grain, furniture, and ranch equipment. He did not know whether Orrie Bean would sell him supplies or not, or whether the price would be reasonable if he did. Perhaps he would have to send Morgan back to Prineville for several more loads before snow flew, but there was plenty of time for that. There was more pressing work to be done these first few weeks.

Quaid had driven one wagon, Morgan the other. Angie rode on the seat beside Quaid all the way up Crooked River. Now she was very tired. Still she insisted that she would cook supper as soon as Quaid started a fire, that it was her job and he must not baby her.

He got the fire going at once while Morgan took care of the horses, and Lynn watered and staked out her saddle horse, a paint that Quaid had bought from Barlow for the girl. According to Morgan he paid too much, but the pony seemed just right for Lynn, gentle but still showing enough spirit to satisfy her, so he did not regret the price he had paid.

He chopped enough wood from a deadfall pine to cook supper and had thrown down his ax when he saw Hank Dawson turn off the road and cross the meadow to him. He was surprised, for he expected Dawson to stay with Matt Runyan until he reached the valley.

He strode toward Dawson who reined up and stepped down. Quaid held out his hand, noting the grave expression on Dawson's knobby face.

"By God, Quaid," Dawson said fervently, "I'm glad to see you. I was afraid I'd miss you."

"What's wrong?"

"Wait till I take care of my horse," Dawson said. "I'll camp here with you tonight."

"Come and meet my wife," Quaid said. "Have supper with us."

"Glad to," Dawson said, and walked with Quaid to the cook fire.

"Angie, I want you to meet Hank Dawson," Quaid said. "You'll remember I met him and Matt Runyan when I was in the valley."

"Certainly I remember," Angie said as she extended her hand. "I'm glad to meet you, Mr. Dawson. You'll have supper with us, of course."

"A pleasure, ma'am," he said.

Quaid introduced Dawson to Lynn who was bringing the grub box from one of the wagons to the fire, then to Wash Morgan who had finished with the teams and was walking toward them, his uneasy gaze on Dawson. They shook hands, then Quaid walked beside Dawson as he led his horse to the river.

"Where did you find this man Morgan?" Dawson asked.

"Rusty Henderson recommended him to me," Quaid said. "Rusty's working for me."

"Good," Dawson said. "Where is he? I thought you had a son, too."

"They're fetching a bunch of horses across from the Ochoco," Quaid said. "I bought some saddle stock from a man named Josh Kinnear. Rusty knows everybody in the country, seems like. He told me about a rancher in Harney County who'll sell me some cattle. I thought I'd better buy a few cows and some young steers I can market in a year or two so I'll have a little income. This business of everything going out and nothing coming in won't last forever."

"You bought the section from Wardell?"

"It's bought and paid for," Quaid said.

Dawson turned to watch Angie and Lynn at the fire. He said, a little wistfully, Quaid thought, "You're a lucky man. I never married, mostly because I go out on jobs like this that are dangerous and I never thought it was fair to a woman to leave her alone most of the time and have her worrying about whether I'd come back. Well, you've got a fine looking wife and a beautiful daughter. A man can't ask for much more."

"No," Quaid agreed.

He thought about what Angie and Lynn had said in the hotel room in Prineville when he had told them to stay in town. He turned away, choked up when he remembered the price Angie was paying to be here with him, and how much she must love him to be willing to pay that price. He said in a low tone, "You're dead right. A man can't ask for much more."

"I suggested that you bring your family," Dawson said. "I told you I didn't look for any more violence. I was wrong, Quaid. God forgive me if you and your women folks suffer because of my mistake."

"What happened?" Quaid demanded.

Dawson told him about the meeting and Sloane's death. "I'm not crying over Pete," Dawson finished. "He was a selfish bastard who would have played Wardell's game against me any day if it would have advanced him with the company, but the point is I think it was cold-blooded murder. No one saw it but the three Hendersons, so there's no way to prove my suspicions, but it's my guess that Tobe went crazy after I told him Sloane was a company man. He'd given Sloane a job, so in his mind it made him look stupid or maybe like a traitor to the others. He was hoping to run into you, then he saw Sloane, and chances are he pulled his gun and shot him without giving him a chance. He had to pay Pete off for fooling him."

"Suppose he'd met us?"

"Hard to tell," Dawson answered. "He might have tried to kill you. Or maybe just warn you. I don't know what he'll do now any more than you do. All he said was that you wouldn't stay. He's mean and ornery and brutal, but I don't think he's enough animal to hurt women. He might be animal enough to kill his own son, though. He'll never forgive Rusty for leaving home and going to work for you of all people."

"I think Rusty knows that," Quaid said.

"Then the boy will watch out."

Angie called supper. Dawson said, "Go ahead. I'll be with you in a minute. I've been standing here gabbing when I should have been looking out for my horse. He belongs to Runyan. I left my team and rig with him."

Quaid walked toward the fire, asking himself what he would do if Henderson struck at him through Angie and Lynn. He knew at once there was nothing he could do except warn Henderson and that would be a waste of time. He was sure of only one thing. If Tobe Henderson or his boys ever laid a hand on Angie or Lynn, or hurt them in any way, he would kill them.

When he reached the fire, Angie glanced at him and saw by the expression on his face that something was wrong. She asked anxiously, "What is it, Dan?"

"Dawson just told me that the Hendersons shot and killed Pete Sloane this morning."

Lynn cried out, her hand coming up to her throat. She turned away, and Quaid, looking at her, wished he hadn't said it in front of her. He had forgotten that she had gone riding with Sloane at least once and perhaps had seen him more than that. She had liked him, but she had seen only the best side of him.

She walked toward the river, her head bowed. Angie, watching her, asked, "You never told her all that you knew or suspected about him, did you?"

"No. You think I should?"

"Not now," Angie said. "I'll tell her later." She put her hands on Quaid's arms and looked up at him for a long moment. Finally she asked, "It will be bad in spite of anything we can do, won't it?"

Quaid nodded. "I'm afraid it will."

Wash Morgan heard it and said quickly, "Don't you worry none, ma'am. We'll take care of the Hendersons if they make trouble."

After supper Quaid and Morgan put up the tent for Angie and Lynn, and then sat beside the fire with Dawson, smoking. Lynn had not eaten any supper. Quaid wondered if she had thought she was in love with Sloane. Or suppose she fell in love with Rusty Henderson and he was killed? For a terrible, pain-filled moment he wished that he had stayed in the Willamette Valley. Then he put the idea out of his mind. There could not be any thought of turning back now. He had passed the point of no return a long time ago.

Suddenly Quaid was aware that Dawson was talking to him. ". . . I think I can persuade the company to let me handle this my way. I've got to convince them that the smart thing for the company to do at this particular time is to settle with these people on their terms so we'll be free to deal with the newcomers without having a feud to worry about. It depends on whether my judgment is considered better than Wardell's. He'll raise hell and prop it up with a chunk, but in my opinion he's got to be removed. I may have to act as agent for a while. I don't want the job because I don't like being tied down, but I'll take it long enough to get this settled."

He knocked his pipe out against his heel and filled it again. He went on, "I'm going to Bend and I'll stay there till I get a decision. Either way I'll let you know. It will consume some time because you can't argue a case by telegraph and it may take several letters. Meanwhile it's hard to tell what Wardell will do, but with Sloane out of the picture I doubt that he will do anything."

He lighted his pipe with a flaming twig from

the fire and pulled on it for a moment, his gaze on Quaid. He said, "Just one more thing. The offer I made was on the basis that the valley people would accept you and anyone else who buys from the company. They agreed to that, but we can count on Henderson trying to intimidate them. I'm not sure he'll succeed. Once you're in the valley you'll just have to play it by ear."

"We don't need them," Wash Morgan said angrily. "Hell, Dawson, this is what's wrong, trying to be friendly with the rest of the settlers. We'll be better off if they let us alone. From what I hear, we can haul supplies cheaper from Prineville than we can buy 'em from Orrie Bean. I ain't afraid to go after 'em, neither."

Dawson grinned around the stem of his pipe. "You've got a good man there, Quaid."

"I think so, too," Quaid said.

They were up at dawn. It would be a long, slow haul through the Narrows to the valley floor, and he wanted to reach his place before dark. Dawson waited until they were loaded and ready to roll. He shook hands with all four of them, and said, "You won't see me until this is settled, one way or the other. Meanwhile look sharp."

"We aim to," Quaid said.

For a moment Dawson's gaze was fixed on Angie's face. She smiled at him and said, "Good luck, Mr. Dawson."

"Thank you," he said, and tipped his hat to her,

a strange but gallant gesture from this tough, red-bearded gnome of a man. Then he wheeled his horse and took the downriver road.

"What a funny man," Angie said. "And to think he's a lawyer and a representative of a big land company."

"I'd trust him all the way," Quaid said, "and that's more than I would say for Sam Wardell."

They took nearly all of the morning to get through the Narrows. The day was a hot one, with no breeze between the high, steep cliffs. The horses had to be stopped and rested often, and although Lynn chafed at the delay, Quaid refused to let her go on ahead.

They nooned when they reached the valley, eating dinner under a limby cottonwood beside the creek. Here a breeze stirred the air. Angie didn't say anything about the valley for a long time. After they finished eating, she stood up, her gaze swinging around the great bowl that lay before her, following the high rimrock on her left to where it became lower far up the valley and moved on past the timbered hills of the Blue Mountains and around to the rim on the other side.

"It's magnificent, Dan," she said. "It's no wonder you fell in love with it. I've never seen anything like it." She looked at him, smiling a little as she added, "You must have some kind of supernatural power."

"Why?"

"You dreamed about it," she said, "and then you came right to it. Isn't that right?"

"In a way," he said, and put an arm around her and hugged her, a great weight dropping from him, for he had known that life would be unbearable if she had not liked the valley.

They went on, passing one ranch after another, and then the settlement. Orrie Bean stayed inside, either not seeing them or choosing to ignore them. No life was evident, not even a horse hitched to the rail. Late in the afternoon they reached the land he had bought.

"You and Lynn will have to live in the tent for a while," he said. "The cabin is pretty bad, but I think we can clean it up."

But a few minutes later he topped a ridge and saw that there was no cabin, just a pile of ashes. Quaid stepped down from the seat, cursing Tobe Henderson and knowing that this was something he should have expected. He stopped, suddenly realizing this was not the way to act in front of the others. He held his arms up to Angie, grinning at her as he said, "Like I told you, you and Lynn will have to live in the tent for a while. You wouldn't have liked that old tumbled-down cabin anyhow."

Angie tried to smile, but she could not. Lynn started to cry, then whirled her horse and rode down to the creek. Quaid looked at Wash Morgan and saw the hard line of his mouth, and heard him say, "They'll pay, Mr. Quaid. We'll see that they do."

He nodded, telling himself that they would indeed.

Chapter 21

QUAID and Wash Morgan took turns standing guard that night. Whatever illusions Quaid had harbored about starting his ranch in peace as a result of Dawson's deal with the settlers were now destroyed. But by sunup nothing had happened. He built a fire and presently when Angie came out of her tent to start breakfast, he saw the deep lines of fatigue in her face and the weight of guilt that descended upon him was almost unbearable.

He went to her and held her in his arms for a moment, then he said, "Let me take you back to Prineville where you'll be safe, you and Lynn."

"No." She stiffened and pulled away from him. "We've made our decision. We will not change it."

He let it go, knowing there was no use to push it. Later in the day Johnny and Rusty arrived with the horses. They had held them at Matt Runyan's place the night before. The old man had ridden along with him. Quaid introduced him to Angie and Lynn, and then Wash Morgan.

For a long moment Runyan stood staring at the pile of ashes that had been the cabin, very tall and straight. His right hand that was raised to his mouth was gently twisting the end of his mustache. Finally he asked, "This Henderson work?"

"Who else would do it?"

"Yes, who else would do such a thing," he said sorrowfully. "There is no experience in life as torturing as to know you have worked and prayed to remove a malignant growth from the heart of a community, and then find it is still there after you have done everything you can."

They all heard him and no one said anything for a moment. Then Rusty burst out, "You know Pa can't change. That malignant growth you're talking about will be here till he's dead."

"Yes, until he's dead," Runyan murmured. "Well, what are your plans, Dan?"

"Rusty's going to break that string of horses to ride, then I figured on him and Johnny going after some cattle for me." Quaid nodded at the pile of ashes. "But that changed my plans a little. I guess we'll start bringing down logs right away for a cabin and we'll get some corrals built."

"Good," Runyan said. "I'd like to work for you if you will hire me. I'm a fairly good hand with tools, and I have Hank Dawson's team we can use to help snake down the logs."

"You're hired," Quaid said.

He was surprised and relieved that the old man wanted to work. Still, he knew he should not have been surprised. He was, as Sam Wardell had said, a guinea pig for the company. More than that, he was also Matt Runyan's guinea pig by which he had hoped to remove the malignant growth from the heart of the community.

For years the old man had, in one way or another, averted serious violence that would have meant tragedy for the settlers. Now Pete Sloane was dead. Runyan knew that there would be more deaths, Quaid thought; that it was only a question of time until the Hendersons would die, or Quaid or Johnny or Rusty or all of them. Runyan wanted to be here when it started, the hope still in him that he could somehow change the course of destiny and avert the blood-letting that now seemed so certain.

"There is one settler named Pat O'Brien who has no family and will not be intimidated," Runyan said. "He's a good worker and he'd be glad to have a job if you want more men."

"I'll hire anyone who wants to work," Quaid said.

"Then I'll ride over and see him," Runyan said.

O'Brien showed up that night, bringing his bedroll, a Winchester, and an axe. Runyan introduced him to everyone in the Quaid party except Rusty who knew him. He shuffled uneasily, glancing at Rusty who sensed what was in his mind, for he said bluntly, "Speak out, Pat. I've gone over to the enemy. I don't reckon Pa knows it yet, but when he does, he'll come a-smoking."

"Why hell, he wouldn't . . . ," O'Brien began uneasily.

"Sure he would," Rusty said, "and you know it. He never changed his mind or backed off from anything in his life. When he hears I'm here he'll make it plain. Either I go home so he can take a blacksnake to me, or he'll hunt me down and shoot me."

They were all startled by his plain words, most of all Lynn, who stared at him wide-eyed. Finally Angie said, "I haven't seen your father, Rusty, but it isn't reasonable that he'd shoot down his own son."

"No, it ain't reasonable, Mrs. Quaid," Rusty said, "but you see, Pa ain't reasonable."

"He's right," Runyan said and turned to Quaid. "Dan, I'd like to suggest that you arrange for all of us to take a turn at standing guard. It may be quite a while before anything happens, but when it does, I would not like for us to be surprised."

"I plan to," Quaid said.

A few minutes later Lynn and Rusty slipped away into the darkness. Angie went to bed, and then O'Brien said, "I've been wanting to talk to you when the women ain't around, Mr. Quaid. Matt here is likely gonna say that it'll all work out nice and peaceable, but I don't think so. You'd better know how it is. Dawson made his offer and we all agreed to take it but Tobe. One thing Dawson said was that part of the deal was for us to stop feuding with you or anyone else who bought land from the company. That's fine and dandy. Nobody's feuding, but what Dawson didn't know is that right away Tobe spreads the word that the valley folks better have nothing to do with you if they know what's good for 'em."

O'Brien paused and shot a glance at Runyan who said, "Go on, Pat."

"Well," O'Brien continued, "I've just got myself to look out for and I'm willing to take a chance of being bulldozed by Tobe Henderson. The rest of 'em are tired of it, too, but they've got wives and kids, and they're afraid to go agin Tobe on account of his threatening 'em like he done. Now Orrie Bean did have guts enough to stand up in meeting and get Tobe out of there, but there was others on hand to back him up and he figured on that. Living and working on a ranch off by yourself and having your wife and kids away from where you are is too much. Even Orrie's backed down now.

"All I'm saying, Mr. Quaid, is that you can't figure on having neighbors in the valley. Nobody's gonna raise a hand to help you, not even if Matt here told 'em to. If Sam Wardell rode in here tonight and Tobe set out to hang him, Matt couldn't stop it. Not now he couldn't, and that's the truth."

"I think it is," Runyan said slowly. "From the time Tobe's father died, I've been the leader in the valley, but I'm an old man now. It is a sad commentary on human beings and their relationship that in the final analysis all of my preaching about peace and brotherly love is as nothing when you stack it up against the physical power and brutality of Tobe Henderson."

O'Brien nodded. "That's about the size of it. Billy Mason, he came in and asked some questions and left. He didn't even try to arrest Tobe for Pete Sloane's murder. I don't figure anybody will help Tobe, but they won't help you, neither."

"I didn't expect it," Quaid said. "If I've got the loyalty of every man here, we'll be strong enough to handle them."

Rusty was still gone, but the rest were sitting around the fire. Quaid's gaze was fixed on Johnny who was taking this in as if it were the big adventure of a lifetime, and that, Quaid thought, was exactly what it was. His eyes moved to Wash Morgan, then Runyan, and finally O'Brien. One traitor could deliver them all into the hands of the Hendersons: but he could not believe that any of them were traitors.

"I reckon none of us are gonna sell you out," Wash Morgan said. "I know what it is to get my guts kicked out of me by the Hendersons. It's like I told you. I wouldn't have signed on with you if I didn't have an axe to grind. Rusty's the same way, only he's had it time after time, so I guess he's got more reason than anybody to hate his Pa. Johnny's your own boy. Runyan ain't a man to go back on his principles. That leaves O'Brien."

"Yeah," O'Brien said. "That leaves me. Well, Morgan, I've had my guts kicked out, too. More recent than you. I talked up at the meeting. Tobe was gone, but he heard about it. He caught me at the store where folks would see what he done to me and spread the word."

O'Brien peeled off his shirt and showed the blue bruises on his ribs. "I wasn't no match for him. He didn't put no marks on my face, but he got me down and kicked hell out of me and said for that to be a lesson to me and everybody else." He put his shirt on as he turned to Quaid. "I'll be a little slow for a few days. My side hurts like hell."

"Take it easy," Quaid said. "I'm glad you told me."

He gave the order for guard duty. Then he waited by the fire until Rusty and Lynn returned. Lynn went into the tent, but Rusty came to the fire. He asked, "What's my time to stand guard?"

"Just before sunup. Matt will wake you." Quaid paused, his gaze on the boy's face, and then he said, "I don't like you taking Lynn away from here after dark."

"We was just down by the creek," Rusty said. "We wasn't far enough away for it to be risky." He swallowed, then he blurted, "Mr. Quaid, I never met a girl like Lynn. You know, I haven't been any good talking to girls before, but I can talk to her. I talked too much maybe. About myself and the way I was brung up and all. I guess I made a fool of myself."

A lot of boys had made fools of themselves over Lynn, Quaid thought. He'd talk to her in the morning. He wasn't going to let her break Rusty's heart. Then the thought occurred to him that maybe, just maybe, she had finally met a boy she wasn't flirting with.

He didn't know what to say, so he let it go with, "She's a good girl to make a fool of yourself over, Rusty."

"She sure is, Mr. Quaid," Rusty said eagerly. "She sure is."

Quaid picked up his Winchester and moved away from the fire, smiling a little as he thought about Rusty who had probably been shy all his life with girls. Then his mind turned to Tobe Henderson and what O'Brien had said. Sooner or later the man would make his move. Time was on his side, time that would fray Quaid's nerves with the waiting, and there was nothing he could do about it.

Chapter 22

THE NEXT WEEKS were the busiest Quaid had ever known. They were all up at dawn. They worked from sunup until dark with time out only for meals, then a short period of smoking and talking around the fire before they went to bed. The thwack of axe against pine and the crack of sledge on wedge and the singing of the long crosscut saw as it sliced the trees into logs were constant sounds those first days.

The weather stayed hot and dry, with only now and then a break provided by thunder storms that boiled up over the Blue Mountains to the north and sometimes would run down Egan Creek, splash the valley with a shower, and disappear on south somewhere across the high desert. After such a shower the smell of sage was strong in the air and Quaid would quit work momentarily and fill his lungs and say to whoever was around, "That's the spiciest smell I ever smelt. I'd forgotten how good it was."

The rain was never great enough to lay the dust for more than a few hours. Often it formed a gray fog that drifted down valley with the wind. It was stirred by the pines when they were dropped and when the logs were snaked down to the building site by the teams and by Rusty who started breaking horses as soon as the first log corral was finished.

Quaid was pleasantly surprised by the tirelessness with which everybody worked. Angie's and Lynn's faces and arms turned dark with a tan they would never have had if they'd stayed in the Willamette Valley. Quaid set up a stove under a canvas to protect it from the rain and Matt Runyan built a long table and benches so all of them could eat together. Johnny was told he had to cut enough firewood each morning for all three meals before he could help Rusty with the horses. This turned out to be the proper motivation, and there was never a day when the women had to scrounge around for chips to keep the fire going. In turn they never failed to have a meal ready on time.

Quaid worried about Angie, for he sensed that their future depended upon these first weeks. If she could make the shift from the comforts of her Willamette Valley farm house to this primitive camping arrangement, then she could surely handle anything the years ahead had to offer.

He slept outside with the men and Angie slept in the tent with Lynn, so he had little time when he was alone with Angie and could talk to her about their problems as he had in the past. In spite of that, he felt she was happy even though she was bone-tired by evening and went to bed as soon as she could.

Quaid continued to keep guards out at night, and during the day none of the men were ever far from their rifles. Still nothing happened. They might have been isolated in a wilderness a thousand miles from another human being. No one visited them. The Hendersons continued to ignore them, and there was no word from Hank Dawson.

One evening Wash Morgan, his patience worn thin by the waiting, said, "Boss, it's crazy to sit around like this. We know what's going to happen about the time we quit watching for it. The Hendersons will hit us when we ain't looking and wipe us out."

"Then there's only one answer, Wash," Quaid said. "We keep on looking."

"There's a better one," Morgan said. "We wipe them out. We can ride over there after dark and burn 'em out and shoot 'em down. I don't see why we've got to sit and wait for them to shoot us."

"No," Runyan said sharply. "That's the Henderson way, but it isn't ours. That's exactly what they're waiting for. If we fired the first shot, we'd put the valley people on their side. The law, too."

"That's right," O'Brien said. "I don't cotton to this waiting any more'n you do, Wash, but Tobe ain't stupid. You can bet he's keeping a guard out, too. We couldn't get close enough to his buildings to burn him out. If we tried, he'd have the evidence he's been looking for. Matt's right about the law. Tobe would go after Billy Mason and we'd wind up in the jug."

"We wait it out, Wash," Quaid said. "At least until we hear from Dawson. I'd like to know what's happened to him."

That was the only time they talked about it, but Quaid knew the thought was in everyone's mind. What happens when we can't wait any longer? The moment was bound to come when taut nerves snapped and the men began quarreling. Something had to be done before that happened.

By the middle of August he sensed that the time had come for a diversion. He sent Johnny and Rusty to Harney County for the cattle he wanted, and the following morning ordered Morgan and O'Brien to go to Prineville with the wagons to bring back the doors and windows and flooring that were necessary to finish the house and outbuildings.

"Don't take any chances," he told Morgan and O'Brien when they left.

Morgan reached down and patted the Winchester that leaned against the seat beside him. "I don't figure on taking any chances, Boss."

"Me, neither," O'Brien said. "Maybe Sloane got killed because he waited. Well, if I see a Henderson I ain't waiting."

After they were gone, Runyan said, "You did a smart thing, Dan, but I wonder what will happen after they get back? I can wait because my way of life has taught me patience, but how about you and the others?"

Quaid grinned wryly. "You're a discerning man, Matt." He glanced at Angie and Lynn who were washing the breakfast dishes and shook his head. "I'm not going to wait all fall and winter to be shot. I keep hoping we'll hear from Dawson. If he brings back a favorable report, maybe we'll separate Henderson from the others for good. If that doesn't happen, we'll have to do what Wash Morgan suggested."

"I would have to leave you," Runyan said. "It would be a mistake." He turned away.

Carrying his Winchester, Quaid walked up the creek to where he and O'Brien had started work on a ditch that would irrigate his meadow land east of the stream. Runyan was right. Such a move would be a mistake. Matt Runyan was the conscience of the valley, and Quaid wanted to keep him on his side.

From a strictly selfish point of view, Quaid wanted to keep Runyan because the old man was a fine craftsman. He was responsible for the walls and roofs and the buildings going together with such tightness and precision that they would last a lifetime. The house had two bedrooms, a kitchen, and a living room. Not far away was the bunkhouse that was big enough to house any crew he would ever need. The day might come when he would be prosperous enough to build a fine frame house, but it would be out of vanity, not necessity. Matt Runyan built for the future, and that was the way he lived.

Quaid had never met a man he respected more than Runyan. But when he thought about the beating the Hendersons had given him that first night he was in the valley, he realized how much truth there was in Runyan's own words that his preaching about peace and brotherly love was as nothing when set against Tobe Henderson's physical strength and brutality.

When he reached the dam site where he intended to take the water out of the creek, he picked up a shovel and, taking his Winchester with him, stepped into the trench that he and O'Brien had started. He planned to throw several heavy logs across the stream at this point, butt cuts of the largest trees they had fallen, thus forming a crude dam which would raise the creek level high enough to force a flow of water into the ditch that he planned to run along the bench to the east. By digging trenches into both banks and dropping the ends of the logs into them, he would have a dam that would hold against the spring runoff.

He threw out one shovel full of dirt when he heard a man call, "Quaid." He scrambled out of the trench, recognizing Tobe Henderson's voice and wondering if his sons had come, too. He wasn't afraid of Tobe, but he was if Shep and Bronc were with him. If they got the drop on him, it might turn out as disastrously as the time they had beaten him unconscious.

Tobe Henderson stood alone on the other side of the creek. Quaid dropped the shovel and faced Henderson, his Winchester in his hands. He asked, "What do you want?"

"To talk," Henderson said. "Put the rifle down."

He waded across the shallow stream. Apparently he wasn't carrying a gun. He must have left his horse somewhere on the other side of the creek behind the screen of willows. He had likely left his gun on the saddle.

Quaid backed up, still holding his Winchester on the ready. He said, "We've got nothing to talk about. You're a coward, Henderson. The last time we talked your boys held me while you beat hell out of me. I suppose they're around here now waiting a chance to grab me again."

Henderson flushed when he heard the word "coward." He said, "Don't call me a coward, farmer. I thought that was the best way to pound some sense into your knot head, but even that didn't do it. You're a damn fool or you'd be able to read the signs well enough to know you'd better stay out of this valley."

Quaid backed up, mentally cursing himself for

his inability to shoot Henderson down, but he could not kill an unarmed man. Henderson had known that. Quaid said, "The signs told me you'd try to run me out of the valley before now."

Henderson put his hands on his hips and stood with his great legs spread, his hands clenched into tremendous fists at his sides. He stood there, motionless and silent, unyielding and unforgiving for several seconds before he said anything. Then he asked, "How do you like it, farmer, working your tail off every day and not knowing when we'll burn you out or give you a smell of powdersmoke? Kind o' tough sitting it out, ain't it?"

"Go get a gun," Quaid said. "We can settle it now. Your way."

Henderson shook his head, grinning. "No. We'll let you wait it out. Your friend Dawson ain't showed and I don't reckon he will. I aim for my neighbors to see what a son-of-a-bitching fake he is. When they do, they'll be on my side, not old Lippy Runyan's."

That's the way it would be, Quaid thought, if Dawson returned with the wrong decision, or if he didn't return at all. He said, "I've got work to do. Talk if you've got talking to do."

"Put the Winchester down," Henderson said. "I'm not packing a gun. Or maybe you're afraid of my fists."

"Not if you're alone," Quaid said.

"I'm alone."

Quaid leaned the rifle against a tree beside the shovel O'Brien had been using the day before. He said, "All right, get it over with."

"Two things," Henderson said. "First, you're not taking any of the creek. All the water belongs to us who live here."

Quaid shook his head. "Better see a lawyer, Henderson. The water you use belongs to you, but half the creek is going on down to Crooked River. I can and will use any or all of that I need."

The man's beefy face darkened. A pulse began beating in his temple. It was all he could do to hold back his temper, Quaid saw. He had not thought Henderson was capable of playing the waiting game, and now it occurred to him that it had been as hard on the big man as it was on anyone.

"To hell with the law," Henderson said harshly. "I'm telling you how it is in this valley. Now the other thing. I didn't know till last night that that bastardly kid of mine was working for you. You sure kept him under cover. Well, I ain't standing for it. He's coming home or he's leaving the valley."

"He won't do either," Quaid said. "We've talked it over."

Henderson's meaty lips thinned and made twin bulges as they tightened together. He was fighting his temper and losing, Quaid thought. Rusty's leaving home was a tender spot, so tender that he was not rational about it.

"Now, by God, you listen to me," Henderson said. "The kid works for me till he's twenty-one. That's two years yet. I'll give you twenty-four hours to send him packing. If you don't, I'm coming after him. You'd better get your wife and girl out of camp before I do."

Quaid's anger exploded suddenly and unexpectedly. He had it under tight control one moment, and then he didn't. He shouted, "Get off my land, Henderson. You're no man. You're an animal. You walk like a man, but that's the closest you come to being one."

Henderson cursed. The shovel Quaid had dropped lay at Henderson's feet. He picked it up and charged at Quaid, holding the metal end in front of him like a spear. "I'll cut off your damned neck," he raged.

Quaid whirled to one side and reached for his Winchester, but his hand swung above the rifle and closed over the handle of O'Brien's shovel. He had no time to grab again. Henderson was on him. He ducked and whirled away and fell. For one terrifying second he thought Henderson had him, that he'd get the sharp point of the shovel on his neck. But the momentum of Henderson's rush had carried him too far, giving Quaid time to scramble to his feet and swing his shovel as Henderson wheeled and rushed at him again.

Both men struck at the same time, their shovels ringing together, the savage impact of the blow hurting their arms and shoulders. They struck again and again, fighting like two strong men from the Middle Ages with quarterstaffs. The third time the shovels caught. Quaid jerked, yanking Henderson's shovel out of his sweaty hands. As Henderson lunged forward, Quaid brought the flat side of the shovel down against the back of his head, knocking him flat. He got up to his hands and knees, then Quaid hit him on the rump, driving him back to the ground.

Dropping his shovel, Quaid picked the half-conscious Henderson up by the back of his collar and seat of his pants and heaved him into the trench he had been digging. Henderson landed on his belly and lay there for a time as Quaid picked up his rifle and cocked it.

Henderson got up and swayed drunkenly for a time, then he turned and splashed across the creek and disappeared through the willows. A moment later Quaid saw him ride up the slope to the bench and disappear from sight.

For a moment Quaid stood motionless as he thought about what had happened. Then it occurred to him that this might be all it would take to trigger an attack. Tobe Henderson had probably never been whipped before in his life. He'd go get his sons and he'd be back.

Quaid ran downstream to the buildings and

found Runyan working inside the bunkhouse. He told the old man what had happened. Runyan nodded and said, "We'd better be ready." He jerked a hand toward the tent. "Johnny's back. You need to talk to him."

"They just left yesterday," Quaid said. "What the hell?"

"Shep ran into them and he headed for home," Runyan said. "Seems that Rusty thought about it most of the night and decided he'd better come back. He figured Shep would tell Tobe and that would bring things to a head. I guess that's what it did, all right."

"Where's Rusty now?"

"He went to the store," Runyan answered. "He told us to stay here, that his fight was with his family and it had to come to a show-down sooner or later."

"My God," Quaid said, and ran to the corral to saddle his horse.

"What are you going to do?" Runyan demanded, running after him.

"Bring him back if I can," Quaid said. "It's my fight, not his. He wouldn't have come back to the valley if he hadn't been working for me. How long ago did he leave?"

"Must have been half an hour."

Quaid tightened the cinch and stepped into the saddle, his rifle in his right hand. Johnny ran out of the tent, calling, "Where you going, Dad?"

"To the store," Quaid shouted. "Stay here with Matt in case the Hendersons show up."

He put his horse into a run, praying he would not be too late.

Chapter 23

HANK DAWSON was not geared for waiting, so the weeks that he idled away in Bend were strictly hell for him. He wired the main office as soon as he arrived, then sat down and wrote a long letter stating his case. He said that the day was gone when the company could send out men like Pete Sloane and tell agents like Sam Wardell to use their own judgment. In the past their judgment had been to intimidate and even to murder if it came to that. In this case, company policy had worked in reverse and Pete Sloane was the man who had been murdered.

He went on to say that this policy might have worked when public opinion was not a force to be considered, but it was now. Furthermore, the company had gone on record saying that public opinion could no longer be ignored. Although Sam Wardell knew this, he had ignored the fact that there were settlers in Egan Valley who should be on the side of the company and would be if properly handled.

The trouble was that Wardell, as had been the case with the previous agents, had asked a ridiculous price for the nine Egan Valley ranches that were being occupied by squatters. At this point Dawson proposed that the company offer to sell to the settlers for $2.00 an acre in order to resolve a long-standing controversy that would prove disastrous if allowed to continue.

Dawson finished with a blunt statement that if the situation in Egan Valley was to be ironed out, Sam Wardell had to go; that he had made himself anathema to the settlers. He had blundered into the valley and in a high-handed manner had offended the squatters and almost got himself lynched. He would have if Matt Runyan, who had made so much trouble for the company in the past, had not saved him. Either Dawson should be appointed temporary agent or the company should immediately send a new man to Prineville with the proper instructions.

Dawson spent all night writing the letter. He made three copies before he had one which satisfied him. He mailed it and returned to his room in the Pilot Butte Inn and slept until the following evening. He knew that his letter would provoke a battle royal in the San Francisco office. He had powerful friends among the men who ruled the company, but so did Wardell.

In the end it boiled down to which group was to control the company; the old time pirates who took the public-be-damned attitude, or those who realized that in the long run the company would profit if it successfully posed as a corporation which had the public's welfare at heart. Unless this faction won, Dawson knew he would be out of a job, a fact which didn't bother him at all. There were plenty of other jobs. He was getting a little bored with this one anyhow.

For days he heard nothing. Dawson suspected that an exchange of letters was taking place between Wardell and the main office. When he did receive an answer, it was mealy-mouthed and made no definite decision. During his days of waiting, Dawson had spent his time looking over the ditches that were taking water out of the Deschutes to irrigate thousands of acres around Bend. He had seen settlers come in by the hundreds, many of them taking land, so he sat down and wrote a letter that was a scorcher.

Men who brought their families to this country and were looking for farms did not want to inherit a fight with their land. Around Bend there was no fight, but anyone who went to Egan Valley to look at company land would learn immediately what he was getting into. Either this controversy had to be settled along the lines he had suggested, or he was resigning. More than that, the company would have a very questionable future because potential customers would pass up Egan Valley and settle in the Bend area.

Again the waiting. There was nothing to do but fish, and in time that palled on him. The waiting finally ended in the middle of August when a letter arrived advising him that Wardell was being recalled. He was to take over the Prineville office for the time being and make a settlement with the Egan Valley squatters as suggested. He wired back asking if Wardell had been so informed. The following day he received a wire saying Wardell had been informed and would turn the Prineville office over to him without delay.

He immediately checked out of the Pilot Butte Inn and rode to Prineville. He did not anticipate any real trouble with Wardell, for he had known the man a long time and judged him to be proud and arrogant but with no stomach for violence. But when he tied in front of the company's office and went in, he saw he was going to have trouble.

Sam Wardell looked up from his desk, recognized Dawson, and rose. He had aged ten years in the weeks since Dawson had seen him. His eyes were bloodshot with dark circles around them, his hair was disheveled, and his black broadcloth suit, which usually was clean and neatly pressed, looked as if it had been slept in. Too, the cool dignity which Wardell had always worn as a protective armor had given way to a kind of wildness which made him a stranger.

"You double-crossing son of a bitch," Wardell said. "You've wanted my job for years and now you think you've got it."

Dawson walked toward the desk, not knowing what to say. When he stood a few feet from Wardell with only the desk between them, he saw the muscular tic in his right cheek and then he had some idea of the pressure the man had been under these last weeks.

"I'm sorry, Sam," Dawson said. "We have to get the Egan Valley trouble settled and we couldn't do it as long as you're agent."

"The hell we couldn't," Wardell said bitterly. "I had it all set. We just had to wait it out."

"Your methods are archaic," Dawson said. "We can't go on using men like Dan Quaid as pawns or hiring Pete Sloanes."

"Too bad the Hendersons got Pete when they did," Wardell said between clenched teeth. "He went up there to kill you, but he didn't live long enough to do it."

Dawson was jarred by this. He asked, "Your orders?"

"No. It was his idea. He sure had you pegged. He said you were after my job."

There was no use to continue the discussion, Dawson thought, so he said curtly, "I'm going to Egan Valley to get things settled. I'll be gone two, three days. That should give you time enough to move your personal belongings out of this office."

Wardell leaned forward, his clenched fists on the desk. He said, "I've worked for the company for twenty years in a dozen places from New Mexico to Montana and here. I've bought and sold mining property, stage lines, and even railroads. In all that time, I've never been called off a job until I finished, and by God, I'm not moving off this one till it's finished."

"There's no use fighting it, Sam," Dawson said. "I'll go get Billy Mason to move you out of here if I have to. I've got a wire in my pocket saying you have been informed of the move. I also have a letter authorizing me to take over this office."

"I was never notified," Wardell said. "That's my story to Billy Mason and he'll believe me. I'll say your wire and letters are forgeries."

The man was insane. It was as if his pride would not let him accept reality, and so he was creating his own world. Dawson said, "Sam, you've had a long and excellent record with the company. Don't spoil it now. They're not firing you. They're simply recalling you. They'll give you another assignment. You'll see."

"Get the hell out of my office," Wardell said.

He straightened, his hands opening and closing at his sides. He was trembling as if he had a chill. Dawson saw there was no use arguing with him, so he said, "All right," turned and walked toward the door.

He was within a step of the door when Wardell called, "Dawson." He turned, saw the gun in Wardell's hand, saw the flash of fire and the cloud of smoke, heard the roar of the shot and the *thwack* of the bullet into the wall beside him. For an instant he was paralyzed, an instant in which his mind for some crazy reason reached back to the time he had told Pete Sloane that Wardell was not a man to do his own killing.

Dawson jumped to one side as he pulled his gun, Wardell's second shot splintering the door casing. Dawson fired only once, his bullet catching Wardell under the chin. He stumbled back, clawing at his throat while blood spurted between his fingers from his severed jugular vein. He crashed into the wall and fell and lay still.

Dawson waited while men rushed in from the street, Barlow from the livery stable and Langer from the bank, and others. Finally Billy Mason came, puffing and blowing after his long run from his office.

"The peddler shot and killed Wardell," Barlow said. "He had his gun in his hand when I got here."

"What about it?" Mason asked.

"He tried to kill me." Dawson pointed to the bullet hole in the wall and the splintered door casing. "I'm not a peddler, Sheriff. My name's Henry Oglethorpe Dawson. I'm the new agent for the C. and E. O. Land Company. I came here to tell Wardell to remove his belongings. When I left, he tried to kill me."

"A hell of a likely story," Barlow sneered. "He's a peddler, Billy. He put his horses up in my barn when he came through here in July. . . ."

"All right, all right," Billy Mason said. "Get out, all of you but Dawson."

Reluctantly the crowd drifted out. Mason checked the gun beside Wardell's desk, smelled it, and put it down. He turned to Dawson, asking, "Do you have any proof of what you told me?"

Dawson showed him the letter and the wire. "All right," Mason said, scratching his head. "One question. Why did you show up in this country pretending to be a peddler?"

"The company sent me here to look at its Egan Valley property and estimate the value of the land being squatted on," Dawson said. "I couldn't go in admitting I was a company man. Later I talked to Matt Runyan and told him who I was, then I met with the settlers and made them an offer. All of them but Tobe Henderson agreed to sell."

"All but Henderson," Mason murmured as if the name was an evil word. "What are you going to do now?"

"I was headed for Egan Valley to tell the settlers that the price had been confirmed by the main office."

"Go ahead," Mason said. "The whole country will be beholden to you if you can straighten out that mess."

Dawson left immediately, ignoring the stares of the men on the street. He rode as hard as he could, but by sundown he knew he could not reach the valley that night. Runyan's horse was neither young nor fast, and he was worn out. Dawson camped alongside the river, but he did not sleep. He would have given anything to have avoided killing Sam Wardell, but the agent had done his best to shoot him. He probably would have succeeded if Dawson had let him pull the trigger a third time.

Then Dawson's thoughts turned to Egan Valley and he wondered if the squatters would keep their word and buy the land upon which they were living, now that he could confirm the tentative offer he had made. He was sick with the thought of possible failure after all that had happened, but knowing Tobe Henderson and his sons, he had to admit that the possibility was very real.

Chapter 24

RUSTY HENDERSON had been in love with Lynn from the moment she had bumped into him in the hotel hall, or so it seemed to him. He wondered if any man had ever faced a more hopeless situation. He had no money except the few dollars that were left out of the fifty he had borrowed from Matt Runyan. He was an outcast from his family and the community. But worse, much worse, was the fact that once his father knew he was in Egan Valley and working for Dan Quaid, he would make trouble. The way Rusty saw it, he was the one who was putting Lynn and her family in danger.

Still, the danger had not seemed an immediate one as long as the valley people stayed away from the Quaids. The truth was he had not wanted to do anything to break up what was the happiest situation in which he had ever found himself. Dan Quaid was an easy man to work for, Rusty liked nothing better than breaking horses, he hit it off fine with Johnny, and he was in love with a girl who to him was perfection. He wasn't sure she loved him, but she obviously liked to be with him and to be kissed by him, and someday, when he was older and had prospects, he would ask her to marry him.

That was the way it stood when he and Johnny were camped on the high desert and Shep, by sheer accident, saw their campfire and rode up. When he recognized Rusty, he asked, "What the hell are you doing out here?"

Rusty faced him, his hand on his gun butt. He didn't know what Shep would do, but he wouldn't have been surprised if his brother had tried to kill him. He said, "It's none of your business. Vamoose."

"Now hold on," Johnny said. "It ain't no secret what we're doing. We're going to buy some cattle in Harney County and fetch 'em to Egan Valley."

"Yeah?" Shep's gaze switched from Rusty to Johnny. "Now who is there in Egan Valley who needs more cattle?"

"My dad," Johnny said. "Dan Quaid."

Shocked, Shep demanded of Rusty, "Are you working for that bastard?"

"I'm working for him," Rusty said. "You going to stop me?"

"Pa will as sure as you're a foot high," Shep said, and whirled his horse and took off in the direction of Egan Valley.

"You fool," Rusty shouted. "You crazy fool. What'd you tell him for?"

"It's no secret," Johnny said, insulted at being called a fool. "If you're ashamed of working for us . . ."

"I'm not, but don't you know who that was?"

When Johnny shook his head, Rusty said, "It's my brother Shep. He'll tell Pa."

Johnny still didn't see the point. "Well, he's bound to find out sooner or later."

"I wish it was later," Rusty said, and turned away, not wanting Johnny to see he was almost in tears.

For half the night he lay awake thinking about it. Then he woke Johnny. He said, "We're going back. Now."

"What's the matter with you?" Johnny demanded. "We came after cattle. . . ."

"Now," Rusty said. "If you're going after cattle, you're riding alone."

He didn't try to explain to Johnny as they rode through the darkness. Johnny just wouldn't understand. No one, raised in the kind of family Johnny had been, would understand the violence of the hatred that could exist between brothers or between a father and son. Rusty, better than any other living person, knew how implacable and unbending Tobe Henderson was. The last thing he would overlook was Rusty's desertion. To him that was treason, and treason was punishable by death.

When they got back, Rusty paused only long enough to tell Matt Runyan what had happened, then he mounted and started toward the settlement. Lynn ran out of the tent, calling, "Rusty, where are you going?"

He looked back, wanting to tell her he had a date with death, and after he'd died, maybe his father wouldn't bother them, but she wouldn't understand any more than Johnny had. He was tempted to go back and take her into his arms and tell her he loved her, but he couldn't, knowing what would happen to him within the hour, or at most two. So he waved and called, "To the store."

When he reached the settlement, he tied and went into the store. Orrie Bean was moving some cans on a rear shelf. When he saw who had come in, he swore, and demanded, "Where'd you come from?"

"I've been in the valley for a month or more," Rusty said. "I'm working for Dan Quaid."

"The hell." Bean walked to him and studied him a long moment, then he asked, "Have you got any idea what your pa will do when he finds out?"

Rusty met his gaze. "I know Pa better than you do," he said. "Of course I know what he'll do."

"What?"

"He'll kill me if I don't kill him. I want you to go tell him I'm here."

"Oh, for God's sake," Bean said. "You think I'm going to have anything to do with your murder?"

"Yes," Rusty said. "If he comes to me here, I've got a chance. If I go to the T Bar, it'll be three to one and I won't have any chance."

Bean thought about it a minute, then he said, "Rusty, this ain't good. Let's go get Matt Runyan and we'll call a meeting. . . ."

"No, Orrie," Rusty said. "This is between Pa'n me. That's why I'm here. Otherwise he'll go to Quaid's and a lot of people are going to get killed. It had better be me. I figure that a Pa killing his own son will do something nothing else would."

"He wouldn't really . . . ," Bean began.

"He'll try and you know it," Rusty said. "Now take my horse and go tell him."

"All right," Bean said reluctantly.

Rusty remained on the porch watching Bean ride across the flat toward the T Bar. The sun lifted higher into the sky. The mercury in the thermometer on the wall kept climbing. He watched a few cottony clouds drift across the sky above the rim to the west. A dust devil appeared on the other side of the creek and spun away into eternity.

These were his last minutes of life. He did not doubt that. He wished he could see Lynn again. No, it was better that he didn't. Then he thought about the time he had stood beside Bronc here in the store when Bronc had hoorawed Dan Quaid and how in a few seconds it had changed from sport to imminent murder and how he had done nothing.

Those few seconds had changed his life. His father had called him a coward. He had been, but not for the reasons his father was thinking. He had been afraid of Bronc and Shep and most of all of his father, or he would have grabbed Bronc's gun and disarmed him. But he wasn't a coward now. After this morning his father would know that.

Orrie Bean came back and tied Rusty's horse. He stepped up on the porch as he said, "Your pa wasn't home. Why don't you go on back to Quaid's?"

"Did you tell Bronc and Shep?"

Bean nodded. "They were both home. They said they'd tell Tobe. You might have to stay here. . . ."

"All right, then I'll stay." Rusty jerked his head in the direction of the T Bar. "Shep and Bronc are coming. Looks like they don't figure to wait for Pa."

"Oh hell," Bean said in exasperation and, walking past Rusty, went to the back of the store, took a Winchester from the gun rack, and loaded it. He returned to the front of the store and stood in the doorway and leaned the rifle against the wall.

Rusty waited until his brothers were just beyond the schoolhouse. Then he stepped off the porch, his right hand close to the butt of his gun. They would stop and get off their horses, he thought, and come at him from two sides. He might beat one of them to the draw but not the two of them. They liked a sure bet if they could arrange it. That was something their father had taught them.

On the other side of the schoolhouse they split, Shep pulling up and dismounting, Bronc disappearing behind the schoolhouse. Shep walked toward Rusty, calling, "You coming home or ain't you?"

"No," Rusty said. "I told Orrie to tell Pa I was here."

Shep stopped and, reaching for paper and tobacco, lazily rolled a cigarette. He said, "Come on and get on your horse, kid. Pa wasn't home but he'll be along purty soon. He'll sure be glad to see you."

Rusty stood staring at Shep, uncertain. Shep didn't act as if he aimed to go for his gun, but Bronc wasn't in sight. Rusty said, "What'd you come for? You knew damned well I wouldn't go back with . . ."

Bronc fired from the corner of the school-house. Rusty felt the hammer blow of the slug high in his chest. He reached for his gun, but his hand found nothing. He was falling and falling into a great, black well that had no depth.

"Got him," Bronc yelled in triumph. "Just like shooting fish in a barrel."

"I'll finish him," Shep said, dropping his cigarette and reaching for his gun.

Orrie Bean sighed and picked up his rifle. Like

Matt Runyan and Pat O'Brien, he had reached the parting of the ways. This was the point from which there was no return. He shot Shep through the heart. Bronc was ten feet past the corner of the schoolhouse when he saw Shep drop. He yelled and plunged back to safety. Bean waited until he was on his horse and racing across the flat, then he fired two shots to hurry his passage and immediately wished he had taken aim. Now Tobe would be here soon with Bronc and that made bad odds.

He put the rifle back and, stepping off the porch, knelt beside Rusty. He was hard hit, but he had a good chance. Mrs. Bean, hearing the shooting, had run out of the house. Orrie picked Rusty up and called, "Hold the screen open, Ma." He carried Rusty inside and laid him on the bed in the front bedroom.

"Take care of him," Bean said. "The bullet's too high to kill him unless he starts bleeding or gets blood poison."

Mrs. Bean opened Rusty's shirt as she asked, "What happened?"

For a moment Bean said nothing. He wiped a hand across his mouth and thought of all the times he had bowed and scraped trying to keep from irritating Tobe Henderson, how he had finally worked up enough courage at the meeting to back Matt Runyan, and how afterwards all the others except O'Brien had got down on their knees again to Henderson. Alone then, he'd had to talk like hell to Tobe and tell him that he had done him a good turn getting him out of the meeting and that nobody really intended to take Dawson's offer.

Mrs. Bean straightened up. "It ain't bleeding much, Orrie, but the bullet's got to come out. We'll have to get Matt. I can't do nothing for the boy." She shook her head at her husband. "You haven't told me what happened."

"I've walked easy for a long time, Ma," he said, "but my foot finally slipped. I just killed Shep Henderson." He told her how it had been, and added, "I'm going back to wait for Tobe. We'll have to send for Matt later."

He returned to the porch of the store and stood in the doorway staring across the flat at the T Bar. On the other side of the road Shep Henderson lay staring at the sky with unseeing eyes, his mouth open, the flies making a dark cluster on his face.

Chapter 25

WHEN QUAID reached the store, he saw a body lying on the other side of the road. He hit the ground and ran to the dead man, sick with fear that it was Rusty. He made an involuntary sound of relief when he saw that it was Shep Henderson. Rusty was nowhere around.

Quaid wheeled to face Orrie Bean who stood in the doorway of the store, a rifle in his hands. "Where's Rusty?"

Bean jerked a thumb toward his house. "In bed. My wife's with him. He stopped a slug. Bronc got away, but he'll be back with Tobe before long."

Quaid thought: *Rusty downed Shep, but Shep must have hit Rusty before he died. Or Bronc did before he pulled out.* He stared at the scowling storekeeper, hating the man as he told himself he had been hand in glove with Tobe Henderson all the time.

Then, because anger and anxiety about Rusty swept his temper out of control, he shouted, "Rusty wasn't a match for his brothers. Why did you let them shoot him?"

He saw Bean's face tighten, saw a brooding darkness come over it that reminded him of the way Bean had looked the time he had stood by, perfectly willing to let Bronc kill an unarmed

230

stranger. Bean took a step forward from the doorway, his rifle still in his hands.

"Get out of here, farmer," Bean said. "I'm going to be busy in a little bit, so pull your freight before you get hurt."

Quaid did not understand. He said, "Not till I see Rusty."

He ran toward Bean's house, pulling his horse. When he reached the front door, he dropped the reins and ran inside, not noticing the two riders who were racing across the flat toward the store. Mrs. Bean was sitting beside Rusty who lay on his back, his eyes closed, his face so pale that for an instant Quaid thought he was dead.

Startled, Mrs. Bean rose, asking, "Who are you?"

"Dan Quaid. Rusty's been working for me. How is he?"

"He's got a bullet in him that's got to come out," she said. "He don't seem to be bleeding much, but digging the bullet out may start him to bleeding. Nobody around here can do it except Matt Runyan and he lives a long ways from here."

"He's at my place," Quaid said. "I'll get him." He turned to the door, then spun back, demanding, "Why couldn't your husband go after him?"

She didn't answer for a moment. She was trembling, and very pale, and suddenly he

231

realized she was frightened and he wondered why. Then she said, "He's waiting for Tobe and Bronc Henderson to come and kill him, then they'll come in here and kill Rusty. Me, too, maybe. Orrie's done his best to stay out of it, but he couldn't when Shep and Bronc both came after their brother."

What she was saying didn't make any sense to Quaid. He took her by the shoulders and shook her. "What are you talking about? Why would the Hendersons want to kill him?"

"Orrie never was a fighter," she said. "He's a storekeeper, and no man ever tried harder just to make a living and stay out of trouble." She stood very straight, her chin held high and proud. "But he couldn't stay out when Bronc shot Rusty down and Shep was going to finish him off. That's why he killed Shep. Now Bronc knows who done it, and he'll tell his pa and Tobe won't rest till he's killed Orrie."

Quaid stared at her, finding this hard to believe. Yet he had to. She was a simple, unassuming woman, badly frightened and still inordinately proud of her husband. Then the explanation came to him. After being afraid of Tobe Henderson all these years, Orrie Bean, under the pressure of those terrifying minutes, had finally become a man.

Outside a rifle cracked. A burst of revolver fire followed. Mrs. Bean cried out and ran past Quaid into the room across the hall. She was starting to take a rifle down from a set of antlers on the wall when Quaid shouted at her, "Stay here with Rusty," and ran out of the house.

Tobe and Bronc Henderson were coming in fast, raking their horses with their spurs. Quaid guessed that Bean had fired the rifle shot, but he wasn't shooting now. Both Hendersons had emptied their pistols at the store, then for some strange reason made a sharp turn to their left and pulled in behind the schoolhouse.

Quaid was sure the Hendersons hadn't seen him, for their attention had been fixed on the store. He stood in the road in front of Bean's house, trying to make some sense out of the Hendersons' maneuver. They'd been barreling in straight for the store and their gunfire had apparently silenced Orrie Bean. At least he hadn't fired a shot since Quaid had left the house. Why, then, had the Hendersons taken refuge behind the schoolhouse?

Maybe they thought Bean was playing possum and they'd fox him by circling the house and coming in through the back. Or maybe they intended to go into his house and finish Rusty off and make Bean's wife a prisoner. It was a logical guess that Rusty would be in the house if he was still alive, and they'd bring Bean out of the store in a hurry if they had his wife.

The next instant the Hendersons rode around

the corner of the schoolhouse. Bending low in their saddles and cracking steel to their horses, they charged straight at Quaid, yelling at the top of their voices. He knew then he'd been wrong. They had seen him. They must have emptied their guns and had pulled in behind the schoolhouse to reload. Now they had him in the open like a squirrel sitting up on a pine log for everybody to see.

Quaid had no time to think about what to do or to make a run for the protection of the horse trough between him and the store. Both Hendersons were firing. Bullets flew around Quaid as he dropped to one knee and brought the rifle to his shoulder. One slug tugged at his left sleeve. Another snatched his hat off his head. Then he squeezed off his first shot and brought Bronc out of his saddle in a rolling fall. He hit the ground like a rag doll and lay still.

Quaid jacked another shell into the chamber and let go at Tobe who loomed as big as a house in front of him. A clean miss! He'd thrown away his chance and now he was a dead man.

Tobe was close, his pistol roaring, the bullet making a white hot crease across Quaid's left shoulder. Quaid levered another shell into place and fired, then tumbled sideways as Henderson flashed past, the wicked, flashing hoofs of the big horse missing him by inches.

Tobe had meant to ride him down, and he had

not failed by much. When Quaid sat up, he saw why Henderson had failed. He was reeling in the saddle like a drunk and had lost control of his horse. He was trying to turn to fire back at Quaid, but his gun slipped out of his hand. He fell off his horse between the house and the store, a sodden, lifeless hulk when he hit the ground.

Quaid ran to him and dug a toe into his ribs. Tobe Henderson was past the place where he would ever harm another human being. Mrs. Bean raced past Quaid, screaming, "Orrie! Orrie, are you all right?"

Quickly Quaid ran to Bronc, but he was dead, too. When he turned to the store, he saw that Orrie was outside on the porch, holding his wife in his arms, his face a red mask. Mrs. Bean was almost hysterical as she tried to wipe the blood from her husband's face. He was reassuring her, telling her over and over again that he was all right.

When Quaid reached him, Bean said, "I guess I played it like a fool. I thought I could hold them off by shooting through the window, but I only got one shot off when their bullets busted the glass all around me and cut my face all to hell. The blood ran into my eyes and I was blind."

"Better get to the house and have your wife stop the bleeding," Quaid said. "I'll go fetch Matt."

"Won't be no trouble stopping the bleeding,"

Bean said. "A few cobwebs will do the trick." He swiped at his eyes again and peered at Quaid. "You got both of 'em?"

"They're dead," Quaid said. "They tried to run me down."

"Tobe underestimated you," Bean said. "He told me you were just a Willamette Valley greenhorn and you'd soon be gone, but he was the one who acted like a greenhorn. He ought to have knowed a man does mighty little straight shooting from the back of a running horse. He was a fool." Hesitantly Bean offered his hand. "I'm sorry about that time in the store when Bronc was hoorawing you. I should have . . ."

"Forget it," Quaid said as he took Bean's hand. "Looks like I figured you wrong, too. I didn't know till your wife told me that you were the one who smoked Shep down." He turned to his horse, calling back, "I'll send Matt pronto."

He raised a long yell before he reached his corral that brought Matt and Johnny running. Quickly he related what had happened and told Matt to take his horse, then as he turned toward the tent, he saw that Lynn had come up and heard what he'd said.

"I'm going to Rusty," she told him. "Maybe I can't help, but I've got to see him."

He caught her by the shoulders. He said roughly, "Now you listen to me. You winked at me the day you were born and you've been flirting with boys ever since. Don't do it with Rusty. I don't think he can stand it."

Angry, she cried, "You think I've been flirting with him? I love him. I'll marry him if he ever gets around to asking me."

"All right, maybe you'd better tell him," Quaid said. "It's my guess that's what he'll need to get well. He's been through hell this morning if I know that boy. Chances are he thinks nobody on this earth loves him."

"I'll tell him," she said. "Now will you let me go?"

He nodded. "I'll help you saddle up."

Johnny was gone, riding hard to catch up with Matt Runyan. A moment later Lynn was in hot pursuit, her black hair flying behind her. She rode like a boy, he thought as he watched her. This was her kind of country just as it was his and Johnny's. Then he thought of Angie and he felt guilty because she was the last to enter his mind. It shouldn't have been that way.

She was standing in front of the tent waiting for him. He put an arm around her and kissed her. Then he led her to the creek and sprawled out in the shade. He told her what had happened, and added thoughtfully, "I suppose it may be different after a while, but right now killing two men doesn't bother me. All I can think of is that we can go ahead and do our work without worrying about the Hendersons jumping us from the brush."

He took off his hat and poked a finger through the bullet hole. The hat was battered and dirty and sweat-stained. It wasn't a greenhorn's hat any more, he thought.

Angie smiled, a finger of her right hand twisting a lock of his hair. She said, "It will be all right. I knew it would."

He sat up and stared at her. "Seems to me you were the one who dreamed about trouble and suffering and heart aches and death."

She nodded. "What's more, I believe in dreams. They're not just superstitions like I told you once, but I lied to you because I knew we couldn't turn back. Our lives would have been ruined if we had gone back after coming this far."

"But if you believe in dreams, and if you dreamed about death . . ."

"Oh, I didn't tell you all of the dream," she said, smiling again. "You see, we weren't the ones who died in my dream."

He groaned. "You took your time telling me," he said. "For that, I've got to punish you."

He brought her to him and kissed her hard and passionately, and when he released her, she pressed her face against his shirt front, and she said, her voice so low that he barely heard her, "Dan, punish me a little more."